Devoted to Him

Devoted to Him

SOFIA TATE

To Colette —
Ignite The spark —
be consumed...
Peace + love,
♡ Sofia xoxo

FOREVER YOURS

New York Boston

Copyright © 2014 by Ulyana Dejneka
Excerpt from *Breathless for Him* copyright © 2014 by Ulyana Dejneka
Cover design by Elizabeth Turner
Cover copyright © 2014 by Hachette Book Group, Inc.

Forever Yours
Hachette Book Group
1290 Avenue of the Americas
New York, NY 10104
hachettebookgroup.com
twitter.com/foreverromance

First published as an ebook and as a print on demand: December 2014

Forever Yours is an imprint of Grand Central Publishing.
The Forever Yours name and logo are trademarks of Hachette Book Group, Inc.

The publisher is not responsible for websites (or their content) that are not owned by the publisher.

The Hachette Speakers Bureau provides a wide range of authors for speaking events. To find out more, go to www.hachettespeakersbureau.com or call (866) 376-6591.

ISBN: 978-1-4555-5737-0 (ebook edition)
ISBN: 978-1-4555-5742-4 (print on demand edition)

For Linda Judge,
my BFF from Buckinghamshire.
Our love for Duran Duran brought us together,
and you've been my rock ever since.
You always believed and never wavered.
Love you so much! xoxo
#bestmatesforlife

Acknowledgments

The reaction to *Breathless for Him*, the first book in my Davison & Allegra series, was overwhelming. I was so awed and humbled by it all. My rock-star editor extraordinaire, Megha Parekh, always makes sure I do them justice. I'm so excited to continue Davison and Allegra's journey with you! THANK YOU FOR EVERYTHING!

Once again, an ENORMOUS thank-you to the team at Forever Romance / Grand Central Publishing, who are a million kinds of awesomesauce! I must thank Leah Hultenschmidt and Michele Bidelspach for their support and my amazeballs publicist, Julie Paulauski, for everything she did for my debut and creating the hot *BFH* quote cards that just blew me away! Huge thanks also to Jodi Rosoff, Marissa Sangiacomo, Jamie Snider, Janet Robbins for her amazing copyediting, and Elizabeth Turner for the drop-dead-gorgeous covers!

To my fellow Forever Romance authors: Kennedy Ryan, you are my rock! Thank you for keeping me off the ledge with your words and laughter. Lia Riley: you are too cool for words! Shannon Richard, Chelsea Fine, Shelley Coriell, Jessica Lemmon, Rie Warren, Rebecca Donovan—loved meeting you at RT! You are all so awesome! Finally, to Cecilia Tan: Thank you so much for your support of *Breathless for Him*! You are a rock star!

Victoria Routledge, Shelly Bell, Hope Tarr, Sara Jane Stone, and Racheline Maltese—thank you so much for your support!

Linda Judge, my BFF from Buckinghamshire: There's a reason DEVOTED TO HIM is for you. The dedication says it all.

Holly Wright: It doesn't matter that we live so far away from each other, because distance is nothing for us. Love you, sweetie! xoxo

Karen Mandeville-Steer: You've become an important part of my life, and I'm so grateful for that, as are Davison & Allegra. "Karen's Two Cents' Worth" are invaluable! You are a true friend, and I cannot wait to meet you in 2015! HUGS! xoxo

To my RWA/NYC friends: Thank you again for your friendship and support of *Breathless for Him*. Extraspecial thanks to Katana Collins, Julia Tagan, and Alyssa Cole.

Logan Belle: What would I do without you? Can't even fathom the thought.

To my husband, Mama, Taissa, David, Dad and Wendy, Nancy, my family, and my friends: Thank you for being there for me when I need you. I love you all very much.

Finally, I need to thank two amazeballs groups of people who played a huge role in promoting *Breathless for Him*. First, I want to give GIGANTIC thanks to the bloggers who supported *BFH* with their reviews and posts: Karen from *Confessions of a Booklovinjunkie*, Ash from *Morning Books & Coffee*, Carol from

Sassy Ray Book Reviews, Nicole from *Heroes and Heartbreakers*, Logan from *Romance at Random*, Kate from *Home. Love. Books.*, Laura from *Bangin' Book Blog*, Michelle from *Sexy Bibliophiles*, Autumn from *Agents of Romance*, Michelle from *Ms. Romantic Reads*, Kari from *Love Words And Books*, Kathy from *Book Reviews and More*, Julie from *Manga Maniac Café*, Nikki from *Ramblings of a Chaotic Mind*, Melanie from *Up In the Cosmos*, Katie from *Babbling About Books, and More!*, A.L. from *The Avid Reader*, Rosarita from *iScream Books*, Lindsay from *Confessions of 2 Book Lovers*, Lauren from *CherryRed's Reads*, Grace from *Books of Love*, Paige from *Mama Kitty Reviews*, Momo from *Books Over Boys*, *The Book Bellas*, *Bitten by Love*, *A Bluestocking's Place*, and *Romancing Rakes for the Love of Romance*. Thank you SO MUCH for reading *BFH* and blogging about it. I hope you enjoy DEVOTED TO HIM!

And to the wonderful, beautiful readers who bought *Breathless for Him* and posted honest reviews on social media: Thank you for your words, whether they were of praise or criticism. I am grateful for all of them because you are the ones I write for, and I hope you'll continue Davison and Allegra's journey with me.

Devoted to Him

Chapter One

DAVISON

Allegra Orsini is the most stubborn, aggravating, maddening, hotheaded, smart-mouthed, opinionated woman on the planet.

And I can't imagine my life without her.

Which is why I'm waiting for her patiently on her father's sofa, my knees bouncing up and down in anticipation. She's in her bedroom getting ready for her private graduation recital—the redo, the one she missed when she was kidnapped.

That bastard Carlo Morandi died a lucky man, because if the NYPD hadn't shot him, I would've paid someone off to leave me alone in a room with him so I could kill him myself. I would've made sure it was slow and painful, not quick like that cop's bullet. It would've been a pleasure to torture him the way he made my beautiful Allegra—my baby, my Venus—suffer, and her mother before that, stalking her, then murdering her in cold blood right in front of Allegra when she was five. If my damn money could be useful for anything, it would've been for that.

Over two months have passed since Allegra was almost taken from me. I took her to Italy to get away from the media frenzy that was ravenous for any news of her, her recovery, and me. Most of all, I needed time to just *be* with her. We had a huge fight before we left, letting out all our anger and frustration, with me destroying a crystal vase in the midst of it when I threw it against the wall. I never want to feel that helpless again.

That fight actually brought us some peace. It was incredibly cathartic, and from that point on, we were determined to fight for our future together. She's already seeing her former therapist, and I'm going to start having joint sessions with her and Dr. Turner as well to continue our healing.

Our trip to Italy was amazing, especially seeing the country through Allegra's eyes. Her fluency in Italian of course helped us when our rental broke down on the *autostrada* and we had to call for roadside assistance. Even more than that, I loved being able to give her the trip she deserved. I pampered her, giving her whatever she wanted so she could relax and enjoy herself. Anything for her. For my Allegra.

And relax she did. I can still hear her moaning, screaming in ecstasy when I fucked her in the bathtub in Venice. How she rode me up and down, arching her back, on the verge of her body exploding, my cock sheathed in her tight cunt, milking it again and again as she shuddered…

Fuck!

I look down at my crotch. I'm hard as a rock.

I jump to my feet to bring down my hard-on. Thank God her

father is still downstairs in his butcher shop. I start pacing the floor, thinking of less arousing topics like the pile of work that's waiting for me on the desk in my office or my old professor's monotone timbre discussing supply and demand in my undergrad macroeconomics class at Harvard.

"Hi."

At the sound of her soft voice, I turn away from the window.

Allegra stands before me in a simple black dress that hugs all of her spectacular curves, with a thin belt that cinches her waist. With her hair pulled back in her familiar style at the nape of her neck, her legs encased in black stockings and those black stilettos that I love, she is a vision.

But my favorite parts of her ensemble are the jewels that adorn her luscious body. I gave her the ruby ring on her right hand in Venice when our gondola floated under the Bridge of Sighs, which, according to legend, was supposed to seal our love for eternity. She couldn't stop crying when I showed it to her and put it on her finger. It was a symbol of my love for her, the promise of a future together. My eyes welled up as well, seeing how happy she was.

Around her neck is the hummingbird pendant on the chain that I bought for her as a Christmas present because that's what she was doing the first time I met her at Le Bistro—humming like a songbird. Sometimes I think that's what attracted me to her even before I saw her warm brown eyes look at me, sending my heart leaping into my damn throat.

Her bejeweled state reaffirms one thing for me and sends out a warning to the men who would dare approach her:

She is mine.

Before I met Allegra, I was never such a sap, not even with Ashton. Thank God I finally saw Ashton for what she really was—cold, unfeeling, materialistic, none of which could ever be used to describe Allegra. Meeting Allegra has opened me up in so many ways. I laugh more. She makes me want to be a better person. But most of all, I can be myself with her.

"Baby..." I murmur. I drink in her beauty, roaming my eyes over her luscious body wrapped in shimmering black fabric. I slowly make my way over to her, our eyes locked on each other. When I reach her, I cup her face with my hands. "You take my breath away."

"Davison," she whispers.

My name crossing her lips in a sexy tone sends my heart soaring and my cock hardening once more. I'm in awe of her. "You look beautiful."

"So do you," she says, fingering my red tie, then running her hands over the lapels of my charcoal-gray suit. "This is one of my favorites."

I lean in and start nibbling on her warm earlobe, tasting her sweet flesh on my tongue. "Why do you think I wore it?"

"Don't start, Harvard. We'll never get out of here if you keep that up."

She wriggles out of my grip, stepping into the hallway, returning with her coat. "Now be a gentleman and help me with this. My father's waiting downstairs."

If anything is going to crush my libido, it's the mention of her father.

"At your service, Venus."

I assist Allegra with her coat, wrapping her cream silk scarf around her neck. I look down into her soft brown eyes, seeing her love reflecting back at me. Even though I've only known her for a few months, I can tell what she's thinking and feeling just from the expression in them.

"Baby, you have nothing to be nervous about," I reassure her. "You've been rehearsing almost every day. I should know. I've been missing you like crazy."

She laughs slightly at my attempt at levity, a smile appearing on her lush lips.

"You've got this. You're going to be amazing."

She nods. "Thank you. I needed that. Now let's go before I lose my nerve."

She turns around, and with my hand on the small of her back, I steer my love out the door.

* * *

ALLEGRA

Front row center.

He's always there, no matter what.

I smile back in silent reply to the one spread across Davison's face. He gives me a quick wink of encouragement from his seat as I clear my throat. I signal to Derek, my accompanist, who begins playing the opening notes on the piano in my favorite rehearsal room at my grad school, the Gotham Conservatory. I open my mouth and enter my comfort zone. I forget the eyes staring at me and the ears listening for everything from pitch to pronunciation.

I finish the final note and shut my eyes, trying not to let the tears that are forming fall down my cheeks. I open them again to see the entire audience on their feet, applauding with Davison and my father shouting, "*Brava!*"

I bow in gratitude for the applause. Davison is the first to embrace me, of course.

"You were amazing, baby," he whispers in my ear.

My father steps up to me with tears in his eyes. "I'm so proud of you, *cara.*"

"*Grazie*, Papa," I tell him. "I just wish Mamma could've seen me."

"She did see you. I know she did," he assures me.

I nod as he holds me once more. A loud voice announces, "Okay, Mr. Orsini, my turn."

My best friend, Luciana Gibbons, is standing behind my father. Next to her is her boyfriend, Tomas Novotny.

"That was incredible, Alli!" she says. "Thanks to you, I'm a total mess!" I laugh as she wipes her eyes. I watch as Tomas places a hand on her shoulder. It makes me smile in wonder how Lucy was resistant to dating Tomas, but now she swoons over him like a schoolgirl.

"You were *vonderful*," Tomas says to me in his thick Czech accent.

"Thank you, Tomas."

The rest of the audience, mostly the faculty, comes over to congratulate me. When Signora Pavoni, my mentor, approaches me, she isn't alone.

"*Brava*, Allegra! I would like to introduce you to one of my dearest friends, Ginevra Ventura."

My mouth drops. I can't believe my eyes. Ginevra Ventura is one of the last true divas of the opera world. She's known for her passionate temperament and her famous string of lovers that ranges from film stars to royal princes. Her nickname is appropriate—"La Diva."

She is everything I imagine her to be from her CD covers. Her gray eyes contrast against the jet-black of her hair with a widow's peak in the front, wearing a black pantsuit and a matching cashmere shawl covering her shoulders. A clearly expensive red handbag is hanging from her elbow.

She takes both of my hands in hers before she speaks to me. "Signorina Orsini, thank you for your performance. I was very impressed by your voice. You are very talented. We will speak on Monday morning. *Lunedì, sì?*" she asks, looking back at Signora Pavoni.

My professor nods. "You made me very proud today, Allegra. Would you stop by my office then, perhaps around eleven?"

"Of course. I'll be there. *Grazie mille,*" I reply, my curiosity piqued, wondering what my professor and La Diva are planning to tell me.

I keep staring at the two women as they walk away, not even noticing Davison returning to claim me.

He wraps his arms around me from the back, placing his head on my shoulder. "What was that about?"

"Do you know who that was?" I ask incredulously.

"Of course. La Diva."

I watch Papa from afar, talking to her and holding his hand over his heart, probably telling her how much he and Mamma loved listening to her albums.

"What did they say to you?"

"Not much. They want me to meet them in Signora Pavoni's office on Monday."

"So basically, you won't be able to focus on anything until then," he whispers into my ear, instantly arousing me.

"Oh yeah, I'll be completely useless," I joke.

"Hmm. We'll see about that, baby. You ready to head to Le Bistro for dinner? The sooner we get there, the sooner we finish."

I turn around in his arms, giving him a quick kiss. "I love how you think, Berkeley."

Chapter Two

Allegra's head is nestled on my shoulder as Charles drives us home from dinner at Le Bistro. We're slightly buzzed from the champagne that the owner and my godfather, Elias Crawford, sent over to our table to congratulate his talented employee on her successful graduation.

I watch as Charles pulls in front of my building. I look down at Allegra's peaceful expression.

"You awake, baby?" I whisper.

"Mmm-hmm," she murmurs. "Just resting my eyes. Are we home?"

"Yes."

Home. I love the sound of that word coming from her mouth. Hopefully, it won't be long until it actually becomes a reality—sharing the same home with her. I have plans.

She waits for me to open the car door for her, something that's become part of our routine. I wrap my arm around her shoulders and don't let go until we're inside my apartment.

I take off her coat, putting it away with mine in the hall closet. When I turn back around, she grabs my tie and pulls me to her, her lips slamming over my mouth. I suck on her tongue, feeding on its sweetness. Her hands run through my hair, bringing me in tighter.

When she pulls away, I groan with need.

"Fuck me, Davison," she commands.

That's all I need to hear. I sweep her up into my arms, carrying her to my bedroom. She doesn't say a word, and neither do I. We both want the same thing—me inside her.

Once there, we work on each other's clothes, quickly taking turns as she undoes my tie and my shirt buttons, and I unzip her dress and pull the bobby pins out of her hair, letting the silky strands fall around her face. Both of us are now fully naked.

I roam my eyes over her luscious body.

Fuck. She is the most gorgeous creature I've ever seen. And she is mine. All mine.

I pick her up and walk with her body wrapped around me to the bed, where I lay her down and fall on top of her.

She quickly wraps her legs around my waist, her hands squeezing my ass.

"Hard, baby," she orders me in a husky voice. "Fuck me hard. I want you now."

I grunt in agreement because I'm too damn overcome with emotion. I'm dying to taste her pussy and suck on her luscious tits, but right now, more than anything, I need that connection with her, to feel my cock sheathed inside her like a vise.

I slide my dick into her pussy, which is completely soaked. "Oh God, baby, you're always ready for me, aren't you?" I moan. "You feel so good. So fucking wet."

I start thrusting inside her, and she quickly picks up my rhythm. She then links my hands with hers, holding them above her head. We are amazing together, always in sync with each other. And when we come together, it's fucking priceless.

Allegra's body is a work of art. So soft, with her sumptuous curves. I love watching her when I thrust my cock inside her, the way her eyes shut tightly, her lush mouth forming Os with each drive, that angelic voice of hers that turns raw and primal when she yells my name right before coming.

She's getting closer as her muscles tighten, going rigid, grinding the heels of her feet into my lower back. *I do this to her.*

"That's it, my love. You're so fucking beautiful. Come for me," I pant.

Her entire body shudders as her orgasm sweeps over her, yelling my name. I can feel her milking my cock harder and harder until I explode inside her, my entire body shaking from the release.

I collapse next to her, immediately reaching for her and wrapping myself around her, our bodies both slick with sweat.

Her brown eyes open, searing into mine. I love looking into them after I make her come, completely softened. Her full lips are swollen from kissing me.

"Mmmm. Thank you, Harvard," she murmurs, her head resting on my chest. "I know you probably wanted to do other stuff first."

My baby never ceases to amaze me. She knows me so damn well.

"Hey, I was just following orders. But don't worry. It was good for me too," I reply.

"Was it? I couldn't tell." She smirks.

I grin back at her, but then I become concerned when she turns her head away for a moment, slowly shifting back to me after a pause so she can look at me in the eyes.

"Davison, tonight…" she starts.

"Yeah?"

"It meant so much to me that you were there."

"Where else would I have been?" I tell her, astonished that she'd even think I wouldn't have been there for her.

She roams her right hand over my chest. "It's just…tonight was so important, and seeing you there in the front row—"

"Center."

"Yes, center," she says with a lift in her voice, "you are everything to me, and I can't imagine not—"

"Stop, Allegra. Don't even think anything like that."

I hate it when her mind goes to that dark place. But after everything she's been through, I'm not surprised she's still afraid that something could happen to us.

"But you didn't even know what I was going to say," she counters.

"Doesn't matter. I'm here with you, in my bed, in my home, and that's all that matters. Oh, except for one thing."

"What?" she asks nervously.

"I love you."

She lifts up her gorgeous face to look into my eyes. "I love you too."

I kiss her gently on the lips as I tighten my hold on her.

Nothing will ever keep us apart, baby. I promise.

* * *

ALLEGRA

At precisely eleven o'clock on Monday morning, I knock on the door of Signora Pavoni's office.

"Come in," her voice instructs me behind the polished wood.

When I walk in, Signora Ginevra Ventura, "La Diva," is sitting opposite my professor. Both women are holding dainty espresso cups in their hands.

"Good morning," I greet them with a slight bow of nervousness. They're not titled royals, but for me, both women hold just as much prestige.

"*Buongiorno*, Allegra. Please have a seat," Signora Pavoni says, directing me to the other guest chair. "You remember my friend Ginevra."

I take La Diva's hand in mine to greet her. *"Certo. Buongiorno, Signora."*

"Signorina Orsini, a pleasure to see you. Thank you for meeting us this morning," she replies in a polished cosmopolitan accent.

I settle into the chair as both women place their cups on the desk. Signora Pavoni leans forward to address me. "Allegra, I would like to speak with you about your career goals, specifically what you envision yourself doing after graduation."

"Oh. Well, I suppose what every aspiring opera singer would do," I stammer. "Audition for roles, try to get accepted into a festival or post-grad program for young singers with a prominent opera house."

La Diva clears her throat. "Signorina Orsini, do you know that I apprentice two young opera singers every summer at my villa outside Milano?"

"Of course. Some of the greatest talents studied under your tutelage."

"Yes, this is true," she replies in a somewhat modest tone. "I have already chosen one singer to teach in June, and now I need to fill the month of July."

Was she going to…

"When I choose a singer, I not only listen for the potential in the voice, but also in the personality, if the singer is able to convey the role with the body and the mind. What I heard at your recital moved me greatly. I saw great potential in you, Allegra, and I would be honored to have you serve as my apprentice in July."

Oh my God.

I start to shake, placing my trembling hand over my heart as my eyes instantly fill with tears. I'm completely overwhelmed.

"I…I'm so honored, Signora Ventura. This is so unexpected. *Grazie mille!* But I don't have the money—"

"All of your expenses are covered," she informs me. "I pay for everything. *Tutto.* Your flights, transportation from the airport, and your stay in my home."

"I don't know what to say."

"The word you're looking for is '*sì*,' Allegra," my professor interjects, rather insistently.

I wipe my eyes and take a deep breath. "Before I give you my answer, Signora Ventura, I need to tell you something. A few months ago, something happened to me, and I would never want what happened to me to affect you in any way. I was the victim of a crime that received high-profile coverage in the media. I don't want the attention that I received to tarnish your reputation or your program if you took me on as an apprentice. I wouldn't—"

The two women quickly glance at each other knowingly, and Signora Pavoni holds up her palm to me, signaling that she wishes to say something.

"Allegra, I told Ginevra about everything you've been through. And I think I speak for both of us when I say that your honesty and selflessness only reassure us that we made the right choice."

A warm hand takes my right one. I turn to La Diva, who nods and looks at me with caring eyes.

"*Cara*, do you know how many incidents I have been involved in, both voluntarily and involuntarily?"

I shake my head.

"More than I can count with both hands. Among many things, I've supposedly ruined marriages, had an opera director fired, and seduced a young prince under the roof of his father's castle. I find you to be a strong, caring woman who has a great future ahead of her. And more importantly, I can teach you how to use that pain to your advantage in your performance."

I smile at her reassurance, tightening my grip on her hand. "Then…I…I…*Sì*! I don't know how to thank you. I am so honored."

"*Eccellente*, Allegra. I am thrilled that you will be joining me. I will get your information from Signora Pavoni, and I shall contact you shortly to discuss the arrangements."

The three of us stand as I shake both women's hands, telling them "Thank you" and "*Grazie*" again and again.

Before I step through the door, La Diva calls out my name.

"*Sì*, Signora?"

"You recall those three scandalous situations I mentioned to you?"

I nod.

"One of them is true," she confesses with a wicked glint in her eyes.

I smile in return before I walk out.

As I make my way to the subway, a thought stops me in my tracks.

Davison.

We're going to be apart for a month. An entire month.

Chapter Three

I t's on the left, Charles," Allegra directs him.

I smile listening to Allegra. My heart warms, seeing how comfortable she's become around him.

Charles pulls over to the curb. I take in the appearance of the tall four-level Chelsea brownstone with a red front door and small, well-manicured courtyard. My palms start to sweat from the anxiety, my heartbeat increasing with each breath.

My smile hides my nervousness. I hold Allegra's hand tightly in mine. This is going to be our first session together with Allegra's therapist. I've never thought much of therapy. In my family, you just keep everything inside and soothe the pain with three fingers of Glenlivet. But she's assured me again and again that Dr. Ophelia Turner is a qualified therapist, how she'd helped her all those years after the trauma of seeing her mother murdered when she was five. So I need to keep an open mind. This is for Allegra, my love.

I open the door of the Maybach for Allegra. Still holding hands, we take the three steps down into the courtyard of Dr. Turner's basement office. Allegra rings the doorbell, and we're buzzed in.

Dr. Turner stands in the foyer, dressed in some kind of gauzy blouse with a black peasant skirt and a pair of taupe Birkenstocks on her feet, her silver hair done in a braid that runs down her back.

She steps forward and hugs my girlfriend. "Allegra, lovely to see you, as always." Then she turns to me, hand outstretched. "Mr. Berkeley, I'm pleased to finally meet you. I'm Dr. Ophelia Turner."

I nod. "Davison Berkeley. Pleasure."

"Let's get started, shall we?"

I follow the women into a small room that's covered in bookshelves and thick velvet drapes, a Persian rug on the floor, and a Tiffany lamp on a side table. I begin to understand why Allegra feels comfortable here. I have to admit it's very cozy. Sinking into a couch upholstered in fabric that matches the drapes, I settle in and immediately take Allegra's hand, more for my reassurance than hers.

Once we're all settled in, Dr. Turner speaks.

"Where would you like to start today?"

Allegra opens her mouth, but I beat her to it. "Allegra asked me to join her for a session."

"Why did you feel that was necessary?" Dr. Turner asks, turning to her.

I quickly glance over at Allegra, watching as she clears her throat. "A lot of feelings came out after I was rescued...Well, he admitted to certain things that I wasn't expecting him to say."

"Like what?" Dr. Turner inquires.

Allegra bends her head in embarrassment, while I shake mine in frustration.

I reply for her. "I told her I was angry with her because I wished she would've told me about the man who was following her before she was taken."

"It was the accomplice, yes?" Dr. Turner confirms.

Allegra and I both nod in reply.

"So you thought she was to blame for being taken?" she asks me pointedly.

"Of course not!" I roar.

This is going to go nowhere.

My face begins to heat up from my frustration. "Why are we even rehashing this?"

"Good," Dr. Turner says, writing something down in her notebook.

I stare at the good doctor like she has two heads. "Excuse me?"

"Davison, you must have been incredibly frustrated and upset when Allegra was kidnapped."

"Well, that's stating the obvious."

"Davison, be nice," Allegra admonishes me.

"No, it's all right, Allegra," Dr. Turner counters before she turns back to me. "Davison, you needed an outlet, someone to blame for what happened."

Is she fucking kidding me?

"For crying out loud, I don't blame Allegra!"

"Of course you don't. But you felt helpless, and you wish that you could've stopped it from happening. You probably even blamed yourself."

I'm frozen. There's nothing to discuss. I don't even notice Allegra has unclasped my left hand, which had formed a fist, now firmly gripping it in hers.

"Allegra, what happened after he told you?"

I look back at her, now tightening my hold to maintain the connection to her.

"The thing is…" she begins with a whisper, "he also told me that he knew about Carlo's plans to make me his sex slave when he took me back to Italy. He overheard me when I was telling Detective Leary about it."

I take a few deep breaths, shuddering as I exhale, remembering the shock of those words when I first heard them.

"What happened then?" Dr. Turner asks.

"I threw a fucking vase at the wall, okay?" I snap back at her.

"Davison, please."

When I look again at Allegra, her eyes are moist, begging me to stop. I release my hand, trailing my fingertips over her soft cheeks.

She leans her head into my palm, closing her eyes.

"Davison, Allegra, please listen to what I'm going to tell you."

We both shift back to Dr. Turner, my left hand now holding Allegra's right one.

"Neither one of you is to blame for what happened. The ones to blame are the perpetrators who committed the crime. I can tell how much you care for each other—"

"I love her," I blurt out, interrupting her, not giving a shit. "Just so we're clear."

The doctor smiles patiently at me. "Yes, Davison, I can see that. Despite the time that's passed, you're still healing from the incident. And you will overcome this because of the love and trust I can sense you have established with each other. As long as you keep communicating and are honest with one another, I don't see why you won't be able to build a strong, healthy relationship."

I squeeze Allegra's hand while she's nodding her head, her eyes shut, a small smile across her lips.

Dr. Turner glances at her watch and looks back at us, clasping her hands together in her lap. "That was an excellent first session. We're done for today." She rises from her chair, and Allegra and I follow suit.

We walk to the foyer, where Dr. Turner shakes my hand. "A pleasure, Mr. Berkeley."

"Likewise, Dr. Turner. Thank you."

She then turns to Allegra and hugs her. "We'll be in touch," she says warmly.

"Thank you for everything, Dr. Turner," my love answers graciously.

As they embrace, I can't help but smile to myself.

I agree, Venus. I'm thankful you have Dr. Turner. You're in very good hands.

* * *

"Thank you for coming with me," she says to me in a whisper.

We're now sitting in the Maybach in front of Allegra's building.

"Anything for you, you know that by now, don't you?" I reassure her, running my index finger along her tender cheeks.

She nods. "I do."

"Are you okay, baby? You're being very quiet."

"Therapy sessions take a lot out of me," she replies.

"Is that all?"

"Mmm-hmm."

She's totally lying. But I don't push.

"Well, okay, if you're sure. I need to get back to the office. Dinner tomorrow at my place?"

"It's a date, Harvard."

I lean in and kiss her soft lips. She opens her mouth wider, taking my tongue into her mouth, her hands gripping my hair in a tight hold. She starts to moan, and my cock hardens instantly at that sound, growing larger under the fabric of my trousers. As much as I want to tell Charles to take us around the block a few more times, I know that in front of her father's shop is not the best place to have sex with her, despite the tinted windows.

I reluctantly pull away from her mouth. "Baby, you're killing me. Not here," I plead.

She looks at me sheepishly, and nods after a few seconds. "Okay."

"Hey, listen to me," I command, lifting up her chin with my hands to make sure she's listening to me. "I want you so fucking much right now, but I'm afraid that your father has X-ray vision and would be able to see through the window."

She laughs.

The sweetest sound in the world.

"We'll pick this up later," I tell her.

"Promise?"

"What do you think?"

She flashes that wicked smile at me, the smile I adore.

* * *

As the Maybach heads down the FDR to my office in the Financial District, what was unspoken between us bothers me. I know there was something she wasn't telling me. After what she's been through, she needs to know that I would never leave her, no matter what.

We finally reach the Berkeley Holdings building.

"The usual time this evening, sir?" Charles asks me when I step out of the car.

"Yes. But before you go, I need you to do me a favor."

Chapter Four

Oh my God, you're such a slob."

"Give me a break, will you?" Davison snaps back at me in frustration. "Noodles are hard to navigate with chopsticks."

"You're getting sesame sauce all over yourself."

"So? You know what to do."

I shake my head in exasperation, but smiling simultaneously because it's just like what happened on our first public date, seeing one of Manhattan's most powerful businessmen who's always in control looking a total mess with sauce all over his face. As I wipe the sauce off his chin with my thumb, he smirks.

"Closer, please."

I roll my eyes as I inch my thumb toward his mouth. Once I reach his lips, I watch as they open, immediately taking it in, sucking on it as his tongue swirls around and around.

My eyes are mesmerized by the look in his own, hooded with

hunger. It's probably not just because of the sauce on my thumb.

He moans, instantly shooting electric pulses throughout my entire body.

"Davison?"

"Hmm?" he asks innocently.

"I need my hand back if I'm going to eat."

A groan vibrates through his throat, and he releases my thumb.

"Mood killer," he complains.

"I'm starving, okay?" I laugh in response.

He smiles at me as he picks up his chopsticks, but throws them down within seconds. "So am I," he huffs. He pushes his chair back and heads for the kitchen, returning with a fork.

"Dig in, honey," I tease him.

He shakes his head at me, his eyes narrowed. But then in a split second, his face clears and he leans over to kiss me. I can still taste the sauce on his lips.

"Smart-ass," I murmur.

Davison winks at me. "Takes one to know one."

We smile at each other, then continue eating.

We're sitting at his dining room table, enjoying takeout from the Chinese restaurant near Davison's apartment. Diana Krall's smooth voice croons from the hidden speakers.

I finish my sweet-and-sour chicken, taking a sip of my beer. I glance around at my surroundings—the lit candles in their crystal candleholders, the fine china and cutlery, the linen napkins and tablecloths.

Something is up.

"Okay, what's going on, Harvard?"

"What do you mean?"

"We usually eat dinner sitting on your living room floor. We only eat at the table if it's a special occasion."

He takes a deep breath, then reaches into his jacket, placing a black velvet ring box in front of me.

My heart immediately begins to pound inside my chest.

"This isn't it, so don't—" he starts saying.

"I know it's not because it's not the Cartier box," I interrupt him. "And it's too soon anyway."

I'm not freaking out because I know the ring he is going to give me when he proposes to me, if that ever happens, is in his desk drawer, information that was given inadvertently to me by his ex Ashton.

"Open it," he insists.

I flip the box open and gasp.

It's a key.

"Move in with me, my love."

I freeze.

"I can't," I mutter.

"Why?"

I finally glance up and see his face, worried and confused.

"Look, I know it's probably too soon," he stammers. "If it's your father, I'll talk to him. I know he's old-fashioned, and—"

I reach for his hands and hold them tightly.

"I do want to move in with you, Davison. I just can't yet because I'm going away."

His eyebrows furrow. "Run that by me again?"

I smile, hoping like crazy that he'll take the news well.

"I've been offered an apprenticeship with La Diva at her villa in Italy. For the month of July."

His eyes almost pop out of their sockets. "Ginevra Ventura wants to train you? *The* Ginevra Ventura?"

"There's only one Ginevra Ventura." I laugh nervously. "What do you think?"

Before I know it, Davison leaps from his chair, grabs my hands, and pulls me into his arms, swinging me around the room. I laugh with utter joy as he twirls me around again and again.

"This is fucking awesome, baby!" he shouts.

Once he puts me down, he clamps his mouth over mine, kissing me hard.

"I'm so proud of you," he says, his breath panting. "When did you find out?"

"Two days ago. She asked me when I met with Signora Pavoni in her office."

"I knew something was up in the car after we saw Dr. Turner. Why didn't you tell me sooner?" he asks, tucking a stray hair behind my ear.

"I don't know," I pant. "I was in shock over her offer…I didn't know how you'd react…take your pick."

"You can be so clueless sometimes," he says, shaking his head at me in astonishment.

He takes me by the hand and leads me to his living room. He sits down on the couch, pulling me onto his lap. "Tell me everything."

I settle back into his chest, laying my head on his shoulder. "I don't have many details yet. All I know is that she takes a student for one month in June, the other in July. I'm July. She has a villa in Lombardy, outside of Milan, which is where I'll be staying. Room and board are included."

"You'll take my jet," he declares.

"No, Davison," I sigh. I know he loves to take care of me, but sometimes it can get a bit stifling. "She's paying for my airfare."

"I can't go with you, but at least let me get you there safely."

"Will it make you feel better?"

"Yes."

"Fine." I shake my head.

"I just might go with you to check out her household staff."

"Why?"

"For security reasons," he declares.

"'Security'?"

"Yes, my security. Security of mind that you'll be safe."

I can't help but smile at his protective tendencies, tendencies that I love about him.

He reaches over me for the remote to his stereo and presses a few buttons. The opening notes of our song, "Avalon," begin to echo throughout the room.

"Dance with me, baby," he whispers huskily.

"Always, Harvard."

I rise from his lap, waiting for him. He takes my hand and walks us over to the center of the room. He wraps me in his embrace as we start to sway to Bryan Ferry's sultry voice. I inhale his scent, the spicy cologne mixed with his sweat that intoxicates me every time.

"Allegra," he murmurs into my ear, "I asked you to move in with me because I wanted you to know that I would never leave you. You mean everything to me."

"But what happens if I'm in Italy and—"

"Nothing is going to happen. Trust me."

"I do, Davison. I do trust you. I'm just scared, that's all."

He pulls back, running one hand softly over my cheek. "Don't be."

An intense look crosses over Davison's face. "I love you, Allegra." He leans in and begins to kiss me, his hands moving to the back of my head, holding me tight. I pull his tongue into my mouth, desperate for the taste of him, grateful for his unconditional love.

When we stop, I look into his eyes, reflecting his love for me back at me.

"Make love to me, Harvard."

"At your service, Venus."

He picks me up, carrying me in his arms down the hallway, the sound of Bryan Ferry's voice singing the last notes of our song wafting behind us.

Once we reach his bedroom, Davison sets me down on my feet. He tucks a stray hair behind my ear, stroking my jaw with his fingers.

"Tonight, my love, whatever you want, however you want it, it's all yours. *I'm* yours. You own me," he tells me in that rumble that makes me wet at the sound of it.

My heart rate starts to quicken. "Then take me, because you own *me*, Davison Berkeley. Body and soul."

His eyes stare back at me, afire with lust. Without warning, he pulls my T-shirt from the bottom hem. I swiftly throw my arms in the air, watching him hurl the shirt across the room once he's swiped it off me. I unhook my bra, letting it drop to the floor. He yanks me to him, clamping his mouth over one breast, and begins to suck on it hard before biting the nipple. I moan in pain, but then mewl in ecstasy when he laves it to ease the sting.

I need to feel him against me. "Off," I demand of him, and he obeys, pulling his shirt open as buttons go flying through the air. I draw his rock-hard chest to me so I can reciprocate, licking his pebbled nipples, then sucking on them.

His hands grip my head steady. "Oh God…fuck yes, baby." He groans, the rough sound bouncing off the walls of his spacious bedroom.

I switch to his other nipple, devoting as much attention to it as the other. I press him tighter to me, running my hands along the corded muscles in his back, making me even wetter for him.

Suddenly, his raw voice interrupts my ministrations. "Enough, Venus. Need to be inside you now."

Davison turns me around so I'm facing the bed. He tugs down my sweats, followed by my thong. "The bed, baby. Now. Get on all fours," he commands me.

With my pulse racing at his request, I do as he asks. I wait for him, and when I look back, he's rising onto the bed, his engorged cock jutting into the air. I start taking deep breaths to prepare myself for what's about to happen.

As he positions himself over me, his body heat radiates onto my back. He searches for the opening to my cleft, then drives himself inside me as we gasp in the joy of him inside me, clenching him tightly.

"So beautiful, Allegra," he proclaims in a rasp. "Your creamy skin, your elegant back, your silky hair falling all around you. You are a goddess."

I shut my eyes as they moisten from the beauty of his words.

And then they fly open, widening from the impact of his hard body as he starts to pound me, grunting with each thrust.

"Yes, Davison. Harder," I beg.

"Allegra…" he growls between thrusts. "You are mine. Only mine."

I push myself back to absorb as much of him as I can. I'm being torn apart. And it is glorious. He is a god, commanding me, taking me. I revel in the feel of him inside me, the heat from his chest hovering above me. This is what I will remember when we are apart.

He starts to move faster, echoes of skin slapping against skin drenching my pussy. We pant in unison, desperate for the release from the heated coil growing inside us.

The wave crests, and I scream as I milk his cock. My arms start to shudder, threatening to give out from under me. But I stay upright, waiting for Davison…

He follows my release with his own, bellowing raw and rough from deep in his throat. I fall onto the linen sheets, spent and sated. Davison's body collapses to my side, his arms outstretched with one flopping across my back.

"Look at me, baby," I hear his voice whisper between pants.

I pivot my head to see his emerald eyes blazing back at me.

"You okay?" he asks.

I nod. "I'm perfect."

He nudges his head closer to me, a worried look on his face. "That wasn't too…"

"No, Davison. That was *exactly* what I wanted and what I needed," I reassure him.

A satisfied smile crosses his face. "Love you, Venus."

I grin in return, then lean in to give him a slow, deep kiss. "Love you, Harvard."

Completely exhausted, we drift into sleep lying on our chests, our arms entwined.

* * *

DAVISON

I dig the heels of my hands into my eyes, rubbing them back and forth. For two hours, I've been sitting at the desk in my office at Berkeley Holdings, reading reports of various companies that my company's research analysts had compiled on potential investment opportunities in Eastern Europe while doing my own research on the Internet. The fonts were getting smaller in size as I was getting more cross-eyed by the minute.

I open a desk drawer, looking for the ever-present bottle of Advil to take a preventive strike against a headache. As I chase the pills with a bottle of water, I glance over at the photo of Allegra that sits on my desk.

I'd taken it on the balcony of the palazzo where we stayed in Venice. It was the morning after we'd arrived. She was wearing the white silk robe I'd bought for her at La Perla. We'd just woken up. She was looking out at the traffic below on the Grand Canal, smiling at our view, listening to the sounds of the city. Her hair was falling down the front of her robe, still rumpled from our round of early morning sex. I had my phone with me, so I said her name, and clicked a shot of her when she turned to me. She looked so serene, so content, her eyes shining in the sunlight. The Italian Masters would've given their eyeteeth to paint someone as beautiful as my Allegra.

I check my watch and realize I'm going to be late to meet her at my apartment for dinner. Since she's leaving for Italy soon, I want to spend as much time as I can with her. Thankfully, my office is a twenty-minute walk from my apartment in Battery Park City, and Charles is picking up Allegra at her apartment. I start shoving the reports in my briefcase when someone knocks on my door.

"Come in."

"Do you have a minute?"

It's Ian Parker, an associate in our finance department. He reports to the CFO of Berkeley Holdings, Dominic Craig. Ian's been with the company for two years. He's bright, smart, and ambitious. He's also a Bulldog, and my blood runs Crimson, so whoever wins the annual Harvard-Yale game every year has bragging rights for twenty-four hours the following Monday after the game.

"What's up, Ian? I'm in a bit of a rush."

"This won't take long, Mr. Berkeley. I'm looking over the rough draft of the quarterly report that Mr. Craig gave me, and his numbers are way off from mine."

I glance up from my desk. "Aren't you the one who compiles the numbers for him?"

"Yes, but his are over, by a lot I might add."

"Did you talk to him about the discrepancy?"

"Not yet. I wanted to come to you first."

He hands me both drafts. He was right. Dominic's numbers

for our net profits are almost double Ian's. I pass the papers back to him. "It's probably just human error. Someone put in the wrong data. Talk to him about it. E-mail me both of the reports. And keep me posted. But don't tell him you came to me first. It'll look like you stepped on his toes, and he wouldn't appreciate that."

"Of course, sir. I didn't mean—"

I shake my head at him dismissively. "Don't worry about it. I'm sure it's nothing."

"I will. Thank you. Have a good night, Mr. Berkeley."

"You're welcome. See you tomorrow, Ian."

After Ian leaves, I sit down in my chair, mentally reviewing what Ian just showed me.

Even if he is a Yale man, at least I know where Ian's loyalties lie.

Allegra's photo catches my eye.

I grab my jacket and briefcase. My love is waiting for me.

Chapter Five

Did you enjoy her, Rafaele? I told you she was beautiful."

"Sì, Carlo," he said, zipping up his filthy, torn jeans. "You weren't lying. She was a good fuck. I can't wait to have her again."

"Don't worry, mio amico. You will. Now it's my turn."

Once his pig friend left, Carlo laid his fat body over mine. His stale scent made me want to vomit, but I had something more important to focus on.

"Allegra! Wake up! WAKE UP!"

I open my eyes. Davison is holding me by the shoulders, his eyes widened in fear.

I'm covered in sweat. My throat is parched, as my heart pounds and I pant, not able to catch a breath.

"It's okay. It's me, baby. You're with me, safe in my apartment. You had a nightmare. You were shaking and saying things in your sleep," he says to me, firmly and calmly.

I nod in understanding, still not able to speak.

"Just focus on me, okay? Keep your eyes on mine and breathe."

He keeps a steady hand on me, never wavering. I take in the beauty of his face. His piercing emerald eyes. The strength of his jaw. His lush lips, which are curved down in concern for me.

As my heart rate regulates, he begins to push aside the hair that's plastered to my forehead from the sweat.

"That's better. Would you like to take a shower?"

I nod again.

Davison rises from the bed, gently pulling me with him. He takes my hand, leading me into the bathroom. I watch as he turns on the water, testing it to make sure it's just right.

"Go ahead, my love. It's ready."

He takes a step away from me.

"Stay," I whisper.

He runs a finger down my cheek. "I'm not going anywhere. I was just getting you something to drink."

He turns back to the sink, returning with a glass of ice-cold water that I swallow in three gulps.

I hand him the glass and step into the shower. He's right behind me.

Davison positions me, placing one hand at the small of my back, the other on the back of my head as I lean into the hot spray of water. I close my eyes, letting the water fall over me, cleansing my slicked skin, ridding me of the sweat that had latched on to me.

I lift my head, staring into his questioning eyes.

"Was it the same nightmare?" he asks carefully.

"Yes."

"The one where you're with Carlo?"

I nod silently. I place my hands on his shoulders, pulling him closer to me. I'm nose to nose with him, the man I love more than anything, whose love for me is constant. His strength carries me, keeps me safe, and makes me whole.

"Please, Davison," I ask of him.

He leans in, softly licking my lips. I open my mouth to let him in, tangling my tongue with his. I tug on his hair, bringing him as close as I can to me. We kiss and kiss, savoring the taste of each other. I don't want to stop. I need more. I need to feel his love for me. I need his love to wash away the pain of my past. I want his love to make my past dissipate so that nothing is left but us and our love for each other.

I trail my right hand down his chest to his cock, rubbing it back and forth.

I break away from his mouth, long enough for him to see the desire and longing in my eyes.

He moves me to the side wall and spreads my legs. He inserts his fingers into my pussy, and we both moan at the feel of them inside my soaked cleft. He quickly removes them, then takes his cock in his hand and plunges into me.

Pressing me to the wall, he lifts me as I wrap my legs around his waist. He starts to piston me, groaning with each thrust.

Our grunts reverberate throughout the bathroom, bouncing off the tiled shower walls. I want to come for him, more than anything.

I coil my arms around his shoulders, trying to bring him into me as close as I can. I want to feel everything—his hot breath, his pounding heartbeat, his hard muscles holding me up.

I'm so close. My ankles lock as the backs of my feet bounce off his firm ass with every thrust.

"You feel so good, Davison…I need you so much. So fucking much. Make me forget," I pant.

"Look at me, baby," he commands. "Let me see your gorgeous eyes when you come all over me."

Just as my orgasm crests, I open them in time to see the look of desire in his eyes burning back at me. I feel my cream pooling on his taut torso. I clench his cock tighter, desperate for him to share the wave with me.

His body begins to shudder as his head falls back, the muscles and veins in his neck straining against the skin. He shouts in release, a raw, primal cry of ecstasy.

His arms weakened, I release my legs and slide slowly down the wall, my head on his chest, our breaths matching in short rasps.

He lifts my chin with his index finger so I can look into his eyes.

"I love you, Allegra."

At the sound of those words, I finally let out what I didn't even know I'd been holding inside, collapsing into tears that fall onto his chest. He holds me tightly as he repeats, "I love you. I love you. I love you." At that moment, it's what I need to hear the most.

* * *

DAVISON

To get Allegra's mind off her nightmare, I take her to see Mozart's *The Marriage of Figaro* the following night. Seeing her reaction during the performance, I know I've made the right decision.

Every time I glance over at Allegra, she's smiling, mouthing along to the lyrics with the performers, even conducting the orchestra herself with quick gestures of her fingers. I do follow along with the action on the stage, but I am more interested in staring at my love, entranced by her visceral reaction. Watching her makes me feel like I'm alive.

As thrilled as I am for her apprenticeship in Italy, I don't know what it'll be like for me when I won't be able to feel her, touch her, smell her, kiss her, be buried inside her.

Actually, I do know.

It'll hurt like fucking hell, as if I were missing a limb.

A loud round of applause rises from the audience.

"That was wonderful," she exclaims. "But I'm dying for the restroom. Meet you at the bar?"

I lean over and kiss her softly on the lips. "A glass of champagne will be waiting for you, baby."

After Allegra dashes away, I make my way out with the other patrons. As I wait for her with our drinks at the bar, a grating voice assaults my right ear. "Dump the charity case already, Davis?"

Fuck.

I turn to face my ex-girlfriend. "What the hell do you want, Ashton?"

"I saw you in your family box and just wanted to say hello. You didn't answer my question."

"Usually I'd say it's none of your goddamned business, but I'm pleased to tell you that we're still together. She's moving in with me."

"Oh, really? That's going to be interesting, seeing as she's going to Italy."

I can't believe her fucking nerve. I decide to feign ignorance just to suss her out.

"What are you talking about?"

"Oh, please," she purrs like a lioness about to eat her young, wiping imaginary dust off my shoulder. "Give me a little credit. I heard from a friend of a friend that your little Maria Callas is going to Italy in July. What on earth are you going to do without her for all that time?"

A familiar arm wraps around my waist. "We're going to have a lot of Skype sex," Allegra announces.

I fucking love this woman.

Ashton's lips purse together, her eyes furious with anger aimed at Allegra.

"Honey, would you pass me my drink, please?" my Venus asks of me, her voice dripping with a mixture of possession, lust, and total contempt for the blonde shrew standing across from us.

"With pleasure, baby," I reply, smirking back at Ashton.

I hand her one of the flutes, clinking our glasses together. We each take a sip, then bring our lips closer to each other and shut up Ashton instantly with our long, hot kiss.

When we come up for air, we see the back of Ashton, storming away.

"Did I miss anything?" Allegra asks, leaning in closer to me.

"She knows about Italy."

"How?" she asks worriedly. "I know you didn't tell her."

"Probably my mom," I sigh. "She must've told a friend, who told someone else."

"Sounds like your mother needs to vet her friends better."

"Agreed."

A set of chimes sounds to signal the impending start of the next act.

I take our glasses, placing them on the bar. I grab Allegra by the waist and lean into her ear.

"And for your information, we are taking the scenic route home tonight. With stoplights."

"That's my favorite way home," she whispers in return. Hidden from sight, her right hand cups my crotch, rubbing it slowly back and forth. "But since nobody is sharing the box with us tonight, I think we can start even sooner."

Could I possibly love this woman more?

I give her a wicked look, then Allegra simply grins at me with her eyes lit up, knowing I'm about to take her up on her idea.

With my right hand on her lower back, I steer her back to our box. Shutting the door behind us, I take our chairs and shift them farther back from the edge overlooking the orchestra seats below. We take our seats, and I pull Allegra closer to me. I glance over at her, and she's staring back at me, biting her lower lip, anxious as I am for the second act to start. The signature lights hanging from the Met ceiling are hoisted up. We are now hidden in the shadows.

The audience starts to applaud as the maestro takes his place at the conductor's podium. We clap our hands politely, but when the applause dies down, Allegra shifts her right hand to me, placing it over my crotch. Her face is impassive as she looks straight forward. I put my hand on her right leg, slowly traveling up her stockinged leg to her thigh, where my fingers are stopped by a silk garter. We listen as the overture begins. The curtain is raised. All eyes are now on the stage.

I lean into Allegra's right shoulder. I tilt my head to her ear, sweeping my tongue around the tender flesh of her lobe. She tastes so damn sweet. I can sense her shivering as her breath increases, coming out short and fast from her mouth. "I would give anything right now for you to straddle me and ride me hard until we both scream at the top of our fucking lungs. But we'll have to settle for this, baby," I murmur to her with a rasp, moving my hand across her warm belly south to her pussy.

While I sit back and begin to finger her cunt, Allegra's right hand unzips my trousers and immediately burrows under the flap of my boxers. She reaches my hardened cock and starts to gently caress it, using her thumb to spread the moisture around the head. I grit my teeth as my heartbeat begins to race.

I insert another finger into her cleft, thrusting them in and out, over and over. I find her clit and rub it between my thumb and index finger. I can hear her moaning softly, and when I look at her, her eyes are shut, with her teeth clamped over her lower lip, trying to hold everything in, and I know she's dying to cry out in release.

Allegra's hold on my cock begins to lessen as her orgasm overcomes her, spilling over my fingers. Her head falls back on the chair as she pants for oxygen. I slowly remove my fingers. She smiles at the feel of my touch on her, as I grin at her release, the sated look on her face making me shift in my seat.

When I adjust myself, my love sits up, returning to the task at hand—my engorged dick. Her right shoulder bumps into me as her warm breath breezes across my ear. "So sorry. I'm neglecting you."

"Totally okay, baby," I whisper in return. "I know you'll take care of me."

She laughs under her breath. "Always, Harvard."

I groan hearing the lilt in her voice…so beautiful, so sweet, my Venus.

Her right hand starts to pump my shaft faster. I close my eyes, knowing I'm about to explode. My hands grip the sides of my chair. I'm going to come so fucking hard.

It builds and builds when finally, my essence shoots out, and I suppress a growl as deeply as I can into my gut. From out of nowhere, I feel a tissue being used to wipe me off. My Allegra is always prepared, another reason why I fucking love this woman.

Once my breathing regulates and I put myself back together, I wrap my left arm around her shoulders to get her as close to me as I can. She turns to look at me, and we kiss quickly but deeply.

"I fucking *love* the opera," I murmur into her ear.

"I have a feeling you'll want to come more often," she replies huskily.

"Yes. And to see the opera, of course."

"Oh, of course," she replies, nuzzling my neck.

I lean back into the chair with a huge smile on my face, tucking my goddess as tightly into me as I can.

Oh yeah, I fucking *love* the opera.

Chapter Six

*C*ara?”

Sitting at my kitchen table, I'm mentally replaying the scene with Davison and the blonde shrew the night before at the Met.

“Allegra?”

I don't even notice that my father has been trying to get my attention until he taps me on the wrist.

“Oh, *scusa mi*, Papa. What is it? Is something wrong?”

His eyebrows furrow as he points at the untouched dessert on my plate. “That is what's wrong.”

I sigh, knowing I can't put it off any longer. I sit up in my chair. “I need to tell you something.”

He shifts his chair closer to me, giving me his full attention.

“I had a meeting with Signora Pavoni and Signora Ventura.”

“Do you mean La Diva?” he asks, his eyes widening in surprise.

“*Sì*, Papa,” I nod. “They wanted to speak to me about something.”

"What?"

"I still can't believe this myself," I reply incredulously. "Signora Ventura offered me one of her apprenticeships to study opera with her at her home in Italy."

"*Daverro?*"

I can't help but smile at him. "Yes, Papa, really!"

I watch as he springs from his chair, dragging me up with him.

"*Cara mia!* I am so proud of you!" he shouts, hugging me tightly and kissing me on my head.

"Thank you, Papa," I murmur through my tears.

He pulls me back down to our seats, my hands still grasped in his.

"So, tell me everything! When do you leave?"

"July."

"That's very soon. Have you told Davison? He must be so excited for you."

"I did, but that's not what I'm worried about."

"What is it, then?"

I take a deep breath. "Last night at the opera, Davison and I ran into Ashton."

"You don't mean—"

"*Sì*, Papa. *Her.*"

His eyes open wide in surprise. "*Dio mio!* Go on."

"I caught the end of what she was saying to him, asking what he was going to do without me. And as much as I know that he loves me, I'll be away and she'll be here, doing whatever she can to get him back. I'm just afraid of what could happen."

My father shakes his head.

"You know, *cara*, sometimes you can be so…"

"What, Papa?"

"*Pazza!*" he spits out, using the universal Italian hand gesture for "crazy," indicating how insane he thought I was being. He takes my hand in his.

"I'm not crazy."

"I know. Just listen, *per favore*," he asks calmly.

I settle into my chair. "Go on."

"You need to know what Davison was like when you were missing," he begins to recall for me in a steady manner. "He stayed here in the apartment almost the entire time because he knew if someone was going to call with a ransom demand, they would've called me. He barely slept or ate anything that I gave him. He was on his phone all the time, using every connection he had to track you down."

I don't stop the tears that start running down my face as he continues.

"I couldn't sleep either, of course. When I woke up in the middle of the night and came into the living room to check on him, he would be sitting up on the couch, either staring into space or holding his head in his hands."

My fists clench in reaction to my father's confession.

"The worst happened right before they found you. I was lying in bed, and I thought I heard a noise coming from your room. When I went in, I saw Davison lying on your bed crying his eyes out."

I clamp my hand over my mouth in shock, grabbing his arm with the other. "What did you do?"

"Being the man he is, he was embarrassed, of course. I sat down on the bed and patted his arm, just to tell him it was okay. But then he sat up, and just started saying all these things. 'Where is she, Mr. Orsini? I need her. I love her so much. I feel so helpless. I can't live without her.' I put my arm around him, and before I knew it, he was leaning into me, crying on my shoulder. So I just held him like that, letting him cry as much as he needed to."

I choke on my tears at his revelation. "Oh, Papa, do you know that you were probably more of a father to him in that moment than his father ever was in his whole life?" I tell him gratefully, now holding his hands in mine.

"That's funny," he says, smiling.

"What do you mean?"

"He said the exact same thing to me when he thanked me for doing that."

My heart melts. "Really?"

"*Sì.* Allegra, I may have been suspicious of him at first, but now I know he is perfect for you. He loves you so much, as much as I loved your beautiful mamma. I know he will always take care of you and would never do anything to hurt you."

I lean in to hug him. "I know, Papa. *Grazie.* And now, I think I'm going to have that tiramisu after all." I pull the plate toward me.

"*Bene.* Always remember, no matter how old you get, your papa will still be the wisest man you know."

"Yes, Papa. *Sempre.* Always," I say to him with a peck on his cheek.

* * *

DAVISON

The pop of a champagne cork blends with the laughter and up-lifted voices coming from my living room. Frank Sinatra's cool voice singing the best of Cole Porter contributes to the celebratory vibe of the evening.

I'm standing in my kitchen, watching the festive activity in my apartment through the open space. My cocktail party to celebrate Allegra's apprenticeship in Italy is in full swing. I spared no expense, hiring a caterer, a bartender…nothing but the best for my Venus. I only invited her father, my mother, and her close friends. I'm watching Tomas and Lucy staring at the view of the Hudson River from my window, their arms wrapped around each other. Allegra's father is in deep conversation with her mentor, Signora Pavoni.

But my favorite sound is hearing Allegra laughing out loud. I glance over at her talking with Derek Fisher, her accompanist, and his husband, Aaron. Wearing a tight black dress that emphasizes her sumptuous curves that make me hard from the sight of them, her long, silky brown hair falling around her face, she's laughing so hard, holding her hand over her stomach to keep herself in check.

Suddenly, an emotion comes over me that I'd never experienced before. It's foreign to me, but I realize what it is.

I'm happy.

And I'm going to be even happier once everyone leaves and I can fuck my beloved on every surface in my apartment.

I shake my head and smile when this realization hits me. I'd never felt like this when I was dating Ashton. When she made me throw a party, the screeching sound of her girlfriends' voices grated on my nerves, and their boyfriends measured each other's dicks by bragging whose investment portfolio or summer yacht rental was bigger. Being with Ashton brought me no joy or warmth. My life was empty, dull, and mundane.

But now, thanks to one lost glove, I've never been happier in my life because of Allegra. And tomorrow, she's leaving to study with La Diva in Italy for an entire month, and I'll be back here in New York, missing her as if one of my limbs has been removed from my body with a fucking chainsaw. That's how deep I know the ache will be.

A tap on my arm snaps me from my melancholic state.

"Darling, are you all right?"

I look down into the soft eyes of my mother.

"Yeah, Mom," I murmur.

She frowns. "You're missing her already, aren't you?"

"How'd you know?"

"Sweetheart, I'm your mother. A mother knows these things." She smiles at me compassionately. "So why are you in here while she's out there?"

"I was just checking on the food. But now that you mention it..."

I peck my mom on the cheek, grabbing my empty champagne glass and heading out to the bar for a refill. The flute now full, I make my way to my gorgeous girlfriend, tugging her away apologetically from Derek and Aaron with a wide smile. "I'm sorry, gentlemen, but I need to borrow my woman for a minute."

The two men grin widely at me.

"Borrow away, sir," Derek declares, raising his eyebrow at me.

I pull Allegra with me, her grip growing tighter on my hand.

"For crying out loud, baby, would you ease up?" I shake our clasped hands to indicate that I'm close to losing circulation.

"No, I won't ease up. And I was talking to them, Harvard," she mutters through her teeth.

"I know, but I want you by my side when I say a few words to our guests," I whisper into her ear as I lead her to the center of the room.

"Oh, for chrissakes," I hear her murmur under her breath. I don't even have to look at her to know she's rolling her eyes at me.

I reach for the remote to my sound system that's sitting on the mantel, pausing the music. The guests turn to see why Old Blue Eyes stopped singing.

My heart is pounding in my chest, the way I always get whenever I'm thinking, speaking, basically doing anything related to the amazing woman who I know now is the love of my life, which makes me feel like the luckiest SOB on the planet.

I clear my throat. "Good evening, friends and family. I just wanted to take a moment to acknowledge why you're all here tonight. I asked you here to celebrate the beautiful woman standing to my right. My Allegra."

A flutter of claps and cheers bounces around the walls of my living room. Her delicate palm starts to sweat slightly in my grasp. I stroke my thumb over her hand to soothe her. I hear her take a breath and exhale as I continue.

"Tomorrow, she's leaving for Italy for a month to study opera from La Diva herself, Ginevra Ventura, thanks to Signora Pavoni."

A short smattering of applause salutes the part played by Allegra's mentor, who gives everyone a nod of thanks, placing her hand over her heart.

"And as much as I know we're going to miss her, I know this is an exciting, once-in-a-lifetime opportunity for her, and I'd like us all to raise our glasses to celebrate her accomplishments and the extraordinary woman she is. To Allegra!"

A rousing cheer of "To Allegra!" rises from the guests, their glasses aloft, hailing her.

When I shift to glance at her, she is staring at me, her eyes moist, a smile across her face. *Thank you*, she mouths at me.

I lean in, placing a soft kiss on her lips. I break away to pick up the remote, starting the music again.

Before I can turn back to her, her father approaches me. "Mr. Berkeley, thank you for saying all of those lovely things about my daughter."

I look him square in the eye, unwavering. "I meant every word, sir."

"I know you did." He pats my shoulder, giving me a grateful nod.

Suddenly, I need to see her. I scan the room, but I don't see her anywhere. I head down the hallway, checking my office and the guest bathroom. No Allegra.

I walk into my bedroom, about to yell out her name when I hear voices in the bathroom. I step in closer, making sure my shadow can't be seen from the doorway.

"You're not worried anymore about Ashton?"

Luciana.

"Not after what happened at the Met. I staked my territory."

I smile proudly.

That's my woman.

"And not after what my dad told me."

What's she talking about?

"What did he say?"

Thank you, Luciana.

"When Carlo took me, apparently Davison was a total wreck."

What the hell?

"He stayed with my father at our place. He barely slept, and he was always on the phone trying to work his contacts to find me."

I would've done anything, even gone bankrupt, to find you, baby.

"And then Papa found him on my bed…"

Oh shit.

"And he was crying, feeling totally helpless."

Damn it! Why did he have to tell her that? I guess to reassure her that I really loved her before she left so—

"Aww! Money Boy actually cried?"

My eyes pop out of my head.

What the fuck…

MONEY BOY? LUCIANA CALLS ME MONEY BOY?

Oh, fucking hell, please tell me Allegra doesn't call me that when I'm not around.

"Lucy, not now…and yes, apparently, he cried. Just don't tell anyone I told you that, okay?"

I can tell she's not crazy about the nickname either.

Thank God.

"I promise. That was really sweet, you know. What he said out there."

Silence.

I can barely hear Allegra. "Yeah, I know. He didn't tell me he was going to do that."

"He really loves you, Alli."

I do.

"I really love him too, Lucy." I hear her sigh in exasperation. "This is going to be the longest fucking month of my life."

Mine too, baby. Mine too.

"But then you have all that mind-blowing sex to look forward to when you're reunited."

True.

I'm getting hard just from the thought of it, and I want Lucy to leave so I can taste and fuck my exquisite girlfriend in my bathroom.

"Speaking of which, I think we'd better go back. Davison's probably wondering where I am."

I smirk. *Not exactly, Venus.*

"Yeah, Tomas is probably thinking the same thing."

When I hear Luciana heading out of the bathroom, I quickly slip behind the door of my walk-in closet. Once the coast is clear, I peek into the bathroom to see Allegra standing at the mirror, fixing her hair.

"You're perfect, baby. Don't change a damn thing."

She smiles before she glances over at me. "Sweet-talker."

I shut the door behind me, locking us in. I lean against the wood, taking in the view of her in her formfitting dress, her sweet, mouthwatering tits pushed together by the tight fabric, dying to be touched and tasted.

"Davison, what are you doing?" she murmurs, half-anxious, half-excited. "You have a houseful of guests and catering staff."

"Exactly. *My* guests. *My* house. *My* rules. And right now, I want to fuck *my* girlfriend in *my* bathroom."

Within seconds, her eyes turn fiery with desire as she hops up onto the counter. "Then, *my* love, you'd better hurry up before anyone notices we're missing."

Our eyes now locked on each other, I command her, "Take off your dress."

She licks her lips, making me hard instantly. I watch as she hikes up her dress, first revealing the black garters and stockings hidden underneath, then sitting up slightly as her gorgeous breasts come into view, hidden under black lace. She drops the dress to the floor, then quickly unhooks her bra and removes her thong, both following the dress's path. Her body now on full display, she grins at me wickedly, giving me a *What are you waiting for?* look.

Here I come, baby.

I slowly stride over to her, undoing my belt with each step. Once I reach her, I let my trousers drop down to my feet. She leans over to pull my stiff cock from under my boxers, stroking it gently with her hands. My head falls back as I groan from the exquisite pleasure of feeling her warm, soft skin caressing my dick.

"So good, baby. So fucking good," I moan.

Allegra's fingers moving over my engorged cock is pure ecstasy, and the need for her tongue in my mouth overwhelms me.

I tilt my head back up. I clamp my lips over hers, pliant under mine, her tongue hot as I suck on it. Holding on to the back of her head, I knead her left breast with my right hand. Our heavy moans are the only sounds in the room.

My hand travels down to her pussy, searching for it with my

fingers. Once I find it, I thrust two fingers inside her, spreading the wetness inside her over her outer lips, making sure every inch of her is lubricated, fully prepared to be taken by my cock.

I pull my mouth away. "Ready, Venus?"

Allegra's warm brown eyes burning with desire, she whispers to me in that lilting voice of hers, "Yes."

I pull back from the sink, quickly removing my boxers and stepping out of my pants. I lift her up. Her luscious ass fits perfectly in my hands, as she instantly wraps her legs around my waist. I slam her against the wall, impaling her, easily sliding into her like a glove. We fit together perfectly.

Our breaths match, rapid and excited. Her ankles pull me in tighter to her, locking around my waist. Her pussy clamps onto my cock as I thrust into her.

"Look at me. I want your eyes on me when I make you scream my name," I tell her in a rasp.

With her jaw clenched and determined, she looks at me and rasps in return, "I love you, Davison. Now fuck me hard."

Under her command, I pound into her, our grunting growing louder with each plunge into her sweet pussy.

"You feel so fucking good, baby," I growl.

Suddenly, she kisses me, practically bruising me with her lips, turning me on even more. I want her to come undone so she won't be able to forget what I feel like, what I taste like, when I'm miles away from her.

With each drive, we're closer and closer…

Her head snaps back. I can feel she's on the verge. "Davison!" she shouts.

She's coming, her body shuddering, her sex milking my cock

like a damn vise, tighter and tighter until I groan in exquisite release as I burst inside her, my cum spilling down her legs.

I let go of her as she uncoils her legs from my body, sliding her
back down the bathroom wall. She curls her hands around my
head, now nestled in the crook of her shoulders. We stay mute
until our breaths normalize.

"Think anyone is missing us?" she asks.

"At this point, I really don't care."

I hear her sigh in bliss.

The sweetest sound ever.

I watch as she puts her dress back on, then looks at me directly
in the eye. "Davison?"

"Hmm?"

"Would it be okay if we said our good-byes tonight?"

"Why? You don't want me making a spectacle of myself on the
tarmac at Teterboro tomorrow?" I tease her.

"No, it's not you. It's more like I'll be a total wreck."

I caress her cheek with my fingers. "Whatever you want, baby.
And anyway, what we just did, that was a preview of coming at-
tractions for the rest of the evening."

"So maybe I should go out there and feign some yawning."

I kiss her soundly on the mouth. "The way you think,
woman…totally fucking turns me on."

And it always will.

Chapter Seven

ALLEGRA

Even though my family photos are still standing in their frames on my dresser and nightstand and my beloved promotional poster of "Pavarotti in Central Park" is hanging on its hook on the wall over my desk, my room still seems different thanks to the large black suitcase sitting on the carpet in the center. The emptiness in my room is palpable from where I'm standing in the doorway. This is going to be the longest time I'll be away from my home and my father.

A warm hand settles on my shoulder.

"Ready, *cara*?" my father asks.

"I am," I reassure him. "Just waiting for—"

At that moment, my phone chirps with a text. It's Charles, telling me he's waiting for me downstairs.

"He's here."

I grab my purse and Gotham Conservatory messenger bag,

pulling my suitcase behind me. I stop by the front door to check I've got everything. My father hands me a plastic bag, from which I can already detect the scent of a salami-and-provolone sandwich.

"Papa, they're going to feed me on the plane." And knowing Davison, he's probably overstocked it. I smile thinking of my overprotective man.

He shrugs his shoulders. "Eh, it'll probably be all fancy food. This will remind you of home. And me."

I embrace him tightly, my eyes moistening. "Oh, Papa, how could I possibly forget you?"

"It's just…I'm so proud of you," he croaks, fighting his own tears. "And your mamma would've been too."

At the mention of her, I take a deep breath and try my hardest to keep myself in check. "I know. I love you, Papa."

"*Ti amo anch'io*, Allegra." He pulls back. "Now let me help you down with your suitcase."

Outside on the sidewalk, the hot sun is beaming down on me from a perfect cloudless sky. Some of my neighbors and Papa's employees from the shop are waiting to see me off, shouts of "*buon viaggio!*" echoing all along the pavement. I quickly bid them all good-bye, with more food in aluminum foil and plastic bags being shoved into my hands. Being a true gentleman, Charles takes them from me and puts them into the car, with my suitcase in the trunk of the Maybach.

Papa turns to me one last time. "You're not sad about Davison not coming to see you off?"

"No. We said our good-byes last night. I told him I didn't want to do that at the airport."

Papa's eyes turn wet again. He clears his throat to keep himself in check. "You should go, *cara*. Call me when you arrive."

I start to tear up seeing how affected my father is. "I will. I promise I'll call you every day."

"Don't worry about me. You have more important things to do there."

I hug Papa tightly. "I always worry about you, Papa. *Ti amo*."

"I love you too. Now go. *Buon viaggio*."

He gives me two last kisses on my cheek and on the top of my head before he lets me go.

I step into the car, immediately lowering the window to give my father and our neighbors one last smile and wave.

As Charles drives up the West Side Highway heading for the George Washington Bridge, I glance over at the empty seat where Davison is usually sitting next to me. The spicy scent of his aftershave permeates the car, and my heart drops, knowing that as excited as I am for what's about to happen to me, being away for so long from him will be the worst kind of torture.

As we cross the bridge into New Jersey, I take in the view of Manhattan in all of its glory—the magnificence of the skyscrapers towering over the prewar brownstones, the cars buzzing along the highway downtown to Battery Park City, where I imagine I can see Davison's apartment building from where I'm sitting. The city that holds my heart never stops breathing, its pulse alive and beating.

Once we're off the New Jersey Turnpike, Charles heads west for Teterboro Airport, which handles the majority of the private plane traffic for the Tri-State area. I watch as the security guard at the gate checks something on a clipboard, then waves us through.

We stop at a small cluster of buildings, where Charles helps me with my luggage, guiding me into the terminal.

"Guess you're an expert at this?" I ask him, the nervousness and excitement coursing through my veins.

"You would be correct, Miss Orsini," he replies with a smile that slightly eases my nerves.

He steers me to a desk where I check in, handing over my passport to verify my identity.

"Miss Orsini, the plane is ready to go. I'll escort you out," the petite check-in attendant announces.

I watch as my bags are put on a trolley, heading out the door leading to the tarmac. When I turn back to Charles, he has a strange grin on his face. Even though I haven't known him that long, I can tell something is up with him.

"What's going on?"

He shakes his head, the grin quickly disappearing. "Nothing, ma'am. Mr. Berkeley told me the reason for your trip, and I'm very happy for you."

"Oh, thank you, Charles. That's very kind of you." I take his arm, squeezing it gently to let him know how touched I am, smiling back at him. "Take care of Mr. Berkeley while I'm gone."

"I will, Miss Orsini. Have a good flight."

With a nod of my head, I turn and follow my escort to the tarmac where Davison's plane is sitting. I didn't know what to expect, but the exterior of the plane is decorated minimally with one long black stripe circling it and the only lettering on it is its call sign painted on the side.

The attendant leaves me at the steps. As I walk up, a tall

blond man sporting a crew cut and wearing a black suit with a matching tie is standing at the top of the stairs inside the plane.

"Good morning, Miss Orsini. I'm Gerard, the chief steward for Mr. Berkeley's plane. It's a pleasure to have you aboard."

I extend my hand to him. "Thank you. Please call me Allegra, seeing as we're the only ones on this flight except for the pilot and copilot, I imagine."

Gerard raises his eyebrows at me, a slight grin appearing on his face. "Of course. It's just us, Allegra."

Did I not get a memo or something? Something is definitely going on.

"Please have a seat. We're just doing our final preflight checks, so we'll be off in a few minutes. Can I get you anything?"

"I'm good for now, thanks."

I take a few steps into the cabin, staring in awe. While the exterior of the plane may have been simple, the interior is the complete opposite. The leather seats and carpeting are in a soothing shade of cream, while the fixtures like the light switches and door handles are covered in gold. Couch pillows and a cashmere blanket in taupe cover a long sofa on one side of the cabin. Yet I don't feel intimidated by the opulence of the space. It's elegant yet comfortable. The entire plane signifies that someone of means and power owns it, but when you look inside, it's calming and reassuring, just like Davison.

I sit in one of the single chairs by the window when I hear my phone ring. I almost forgot to turn it off.

When I check the caller ID, I smile.

"Hi, Harvard."

"Hey, baby," his deep voice greets me with that rumble I love. "You on the plane?"

"Yes, and it's gorgeous. Thank you for doing this for me."

"Always, Venus. Did Gerard give you the tour?"

"Um, no. I think he's busy at the moment."

"That's all right. Even though I'm not there, I can do this for you over the phone. Did you know there's a bedroom in the back?"

I never sleep well on planes, so the thought of having a decent rest before I get to Milan excites me to no end. "Really?"

"Of course. Why don't you go check it out? It's the door on the right."

"Umm, okay. I guess I have time."

I look up to the front of the plane to scan for Gerard, but he's probably disappeared into the galley. I unbuckle my seat belt, walking slowly to the back. I turn the handle on the door to the right just like Davison instructed.

The door swings open, and I scream at the sight in front of me.

"Ready to fly my friendly skies, baby?" Davison asks me, a wicked smirk on his face, his eyes alive and shining and locked on mine.

I fly into his arms, coiling my legs around his waist. Grabbing his hair in my hands, I lock my mouth over his, kissing him furiously even though it's been less than twelve hours since I last saw him.

When I can't breathe anymore, I pull back to look at his beautiful face. "What are you doing here?"

He can't stop smiling. "I thought I'd go with you as far as the airport in Milan, then fly up to London for some client meetings before going back to New York."

I stroke his face with my right hand. "What a clever man you are, Davison Berkeley."

"What can I say? I'm the king of multitasking."

"That's not the only thing you're the king of." I grin back at him.

"Damn right, Miss Orsini."

I unwrap my legs as he puts me back down on the floor, where I can finally take a look at him and my surroundings. He looks so hot, his dark hair all rumpled thanks to my eager hands, dressed in a white button-down shirt, the pushed-up sleeves revealing his corded forearms, worn blue jeans, and the brown driving shoes I love on him. In the bedroom, the same color palette of cream and gold decorates the walls and fixtures, save for one thing—the double bed in the middle of the room that's covered in a black cashmere duvet.

"Wow. That looks…comfortable," I comment, envisioning the events to come later in the flight with great anticipation.

"Oh, it is, my love. Very comfortable," he assures me slyly, planting a kiss on my hand before taking it in his, leading me out the door. "Come on. It's almost time to take off."

"So, wait. I'm guessing that I was the last to know that you were planning this, judging by the mischievous looks that Charles and Gerard were giving me."

Davison sits me down in the seat next to his. "Pretty much," he confirms as he's locking his seat belt.

I give him a long stare. "Evil. Pure evil."

He takes my hand again, stroking it with his thumb in that way of his that always arouses me. "But you love it, baby."

I bite down on my lower lip as I shake my head.

I hate it when he's right.

"Yes," I finally admit reluctantly.

Before he can reply with a snarky comment, the captain comes on over the PA system. "Mr. Berkeley, we've been cleared for take-off. Please be seated."

"Here we go," I declare.

"*Andiamo*, baby." With my hand in his firm grip, I remember he said those same exact words to me when we left the cemetery in Naples where my mother is buried.

I pull his hand to my lips, kissing it softly. He smiles at me. He remembers too.

* * *

Sitting across from each other at the small table in the back of the cabin, Davison and I use the linen napkins in our laps to wipe our mouths after our delicious dinner of grilled chicken with mashed potatoes and steamed vegetables. He made sure to serve my favorite dessert—molten chocolate cake with raspberry coulis.

I lean back in my seat to loosen the belt on my jeans. "That was so good."

When I glance at Davison, a sly smile is spread across his face, studying me, suddenly making me self-conscious.

I quickly pat my face. "Do I have any chocolate anywhere? I practically inhaled that cake."

"No," he replies with a deep rumble that makes my toes curl, sending flutters through my belly. "You're just too fucking beautiful for words."

Just as my heartbeat starts to race and my breathing increases,

Gerard chooses that moment to come by to pick up our plates. "Will there be anything else?"

Davison's stare doesn't waver from my eyes as he addresses him. "No, we're all done, Gerard. Once you're finished cleaning up, you can take a break. We won't be needing you for the time being."

"Very good, sir," he acknowledges with a nod.

Davison stays in his seat until Gerard walks away, then he rises to his feet, stepping toward me. He silently holds out his hand, inviting me with his brilliant emerald eyes.

I follow him back to the bedroom. My nerve endings are pulsing to every end point in my body, my heart pounding so hard I can sense it in my ears, my throat.

"Just give me a minute," I ask of him.

"Take all the time you need," he murmurs. "There's a spare toothbrush in the bathroom. And when you finish, come out naked."

I gulp at his last command, not in nervousness, but anticipation. I step into the en suite bathroom, thoroughly brushing my teeth, splashing water over my face, and fingering my hair with my hands. I strip down and leave all of my clothes on the floor.

When I come back into the room, Davison is standing in front of me, wearing only a pair of black silk boxers and a wicked look on his gorgeous face, his eyes hooded with desire. He's holding a black silk scarf, running the soft material through his fingers.

"And what are you planning to do with that?" I ask, gesturing to his occupied hands.

"Thought we'd try something new," he purrs.

"I love trying out new things," I inform him, eager to see where he's going with this.

"That's why I love you, Venus. Now come to me," his deep, raspy voice instructs me.

With my shoulders thrown back and my eyes fixed on his, I stride to him confidently. Once I'm standing in front of him, he softly kisses me on the lips before turning me around to tie the scarf around my eyes.

"Can you see anything?" he asks, his hot breath on my ear.

I shake my head in reply.

My hand is now gripped in his as he leads me to the bed, sitting me down and arranging me. "Push yourself back until you feel the pillows, then lie down."

Using my hands, I slide along the soft fabric of the cashmere duvet, stopping when I sense the lump of the pillows under me. I place my head down, breathing fast as I wait for Davison's next move.

"You look so fucking beautiful, Allegra. I could just watch you for hours."

"And, ironically, that's just about the amount of time we have," I comment.

"No smart-ass remarks," he declares. "All I want to hear from you are groans, moans, yells, screams, and your voice calling my name in ecstasy."

I nod in acknowledgement, grinning like a damn Cheshire cat.

The plane lifts up slightly, but I don't mind the turbulence. The only thing I'm thinking about now is how soon Davison is going to begin pleasuring me.

Something wet and cold drips onto my chest. Chills run up

and down my skin. A familiar smell travels up to my nose.

"What is that, Harvard?"

He wipes a finger across my stomach where the liquid has dripped. "Taste, baby."

I suck his finger into my mouth, and melt upon contact. It's the raspberry coulis that was served with our dessert.

"Mmmm," I moan, tightening my lips harder around his index finger, determined to suck every last drop of the sweet syrup.

He groans.

I finally release his finger. He moves down the bed. I sense a flutter of air. More liquid is poured onto my body. My nipples and belly are covered in it.

"Davison, just as a reminder, this is cashmere I'm lying on."

"I'm touched you're so concerned about my bed linens, my love. But I don't give a fuck about them."

My head sinks helplessly farther into the pillow and I'm about to say something else when the tip of his tongue starts to play with my left nipple, bobbing it up and down, then running it around my areola.

"Fuck, Allegra. You taste so sweet," he purrs.

I moan in rapture, my pussy soaked with desire. I squirm, fisting the cashmere fabric under me as he starts to travel with his tongue down onto my belly, my stomach contracting, my muscles pushing down onto my cleft, so close to coming from the ministrations of his tongue alone.

His mouth travels back and forth across my torso, his tongue leaving a trail of moisture.

"Please, Davison," I plead.

"What is it? I'm busy," he says as if I'm bothering him.

"I need you there…" I pant.

"Where?"

"You know where."

"No, I don't," he teases. "Tell me."

"My pussy. My clit. Everything. I want to come. Please," I beg him.

"Ask me again. And say my name," he commands.

"Make me come, Davison. Suck my clit," I say through gritted teeth.

"Hmm. I'll think about it," he replies, still tormenting me.

The torture is too much to bear.

He moves to my thighs, nipping and licking. I think I'm about to lose it when suddenly he announces, "It's time to feast."

Thank fucking God.

His mouth settles on my soaked pussy, and I whimper at the feel of his tongue swirling inside me as if he were trying to get every last drop of me. His deep moans vibrate across my labia, making me shudder, desperate for more.

And then, when I sense his breath across my clit, I clench the duvet, preparing myself.

The instant Davison inserts my clit into his mouth, my hips jerk violently. He grips my upper thighs, holding me down to keep me steady. And then his fingers enter me, thrusting in and out.

I can't hold it in any longer.

"Davison, oh God! Don't fucking stop!" I beg of him.

My eyes roll back into my head as my orgasm sweeps over me, my hips contracting despite being held down by the sinewy muscles of his strong arms.

I can't catch my breath, panting as Davison makes his way up my body. He pulls the scarf from around my eyes. I blink a few times to adjust to the light, revealing him hovering over me holding himself up by his arms, his gorgeous face covered by the most satisfied smile I've ever seen on him.

"Enjoy that?" he asks, grinning so damn mischievously.

Stupidest question in the history of stupid questions.

I cough out a laugh, still trying to get my heart rate down so I can thank him properly.

I finally take a deep breath. "Come here."

I wrap my hands around his nape, pulling his mouth to mine. When I finally taste him, I am overcome by the heady combination of my arousal, the sweet raspberries, and his warm tongue. The flavor is the most erotic mixture I've ever enjoyed, and I want more. So much more. I kiss him again and again, finally licking around his lips to get every last taste.

"Well?" he asks, his eyebrows raised inquiringly.

"We'll need to do that again. Soon."

"Trust me. We will, baby. And now…"

I watch as he nudges my legs apart with his knees, reaching down with his right hand. His finger slips easily into my pussy.

Oh God…

"Just checking," he grins.

"Round two. Bring it, Harvard," I urge him on.

Like a hand sliding seamlessly into a glove, he enters me, filling me with his girth. He starts to move, pummeling me with each thrust.

"Fuck, Allegra. So good. Always so tight. I love being inside you," he rasps.

He pounds into me, the intensity increasing with each thrust. When I glance down to see his face, his eyes are shut tightly in concentration, the muscles along the sides of his neck straining against his skin. He's past the point of return, arousing me further, seeing this beautiful specimen of a man in his full Alpha glory only exciting me more, stirring my nerve endings, sending my blood racing through my veins.

His body begins to shudder as he nears his release. He thrusts once, twice, then we come together, Davison shouting my name in rapture.

Completely depleted, he collapses on top of me as we fall into a deep sleep.

* * *

I knew this moment was coming. I'd told myself that I would be strong, but I'm going to lose it any second the longer he looks at me like that, with pure love in his eyes.

About an hour ago, we'd showered, gotten dressed, and enjoyed a late supper of omelettes, croissants, fruit, and coffee that Gerard prepared for us. I couldn't handle anything heavier than that due to my nerves. We'd landed shortly thereafter at the airport in Milan around nine o'clock, and waited for the customs agent and an airport official to come on board for passport control. Once he completed his check, the official waited for me out on the tarmac to take me inside the terminal. La Diva's driver texted that he was waiting outside to drive me to her villa once I was ready to say good-bye to Davison.

But I'm nowhere near ready.

As Davison holds my hands, I speak to his shoes instead of his face. "I put a trifecta of songs on your iPod…"

"Allegra…"

"They're not sad ones, just ones that will remind you of me…"

"Allegra…"

"And when I come back, we'll dance to them together in your living room. And—"

"Allegra, please look at me," he tells me calmly yet firmly.

I finally gather myself and tilt my face to him, my eyes boring into his.

"We'll call. We'll Skype. We'll text. It's only a few weeks," he offers with a shrug, as if it's no big deal.

At first, I'm offended at his demeanor, but then I see his chest rising and falling, taking deep breaths. He's hating this as much as I am. Thankfully, his strong, steady hands are keeping my shaking ones under control, but his grip is growing tighter on them.

"Right, it's only a few weeks," I repeat.

The tears running down my face counter all my attempts to stay strong and not break down. He releases my hands, running his thumbs along my cheeks to wipe them away. Then he clamps my face with his hands, looking straight into my eyes.

"I love you, Allegra. So fucking much."

I press my lips together and nod my head to keep myself in check so I can reply without losing it.

"I love you," I declare breathlessly before pulling him to me roughly, kissing him so hard. His arms coil around my waist, grabbing my jacket in his hands, thrusting me to him as we melt into each other, forming one entity.

When we come up for air, we lean our foreheads together, our eyes communicating what we're feeling inside. No more words are necessary.

"Call me when you get to London," I ask of him.

"I will. I promise."

I give him one last quick kiss on the lips and dash down the stairs, not looking back until I have to get into the shuttle van that will take me to the terminal. When I finally do turn around, Davison is staring right back at me. Standing in the doorway of his jet, dressed in one of his dark tailored suits, every hair in place, his tie perfectly knotted, he is the epitome of power. He nods at me encouragingly, pressing me to go on. I mirror him, nodding in return, placing a hand over my heart. Our eyes don't waver until the van pulls away and we can't see each other anymore.

Once I'm fully out of his sight, I let the tears flow.

"*Siete molto fortunata, signorina. Lui è molto bello*," an older woman says to me.

I simply nod. I become angry at this nameless woman. She probably assumes I speak Italian because she saw my name on the flight manifest, and I want to reply to her in Italian, "Yes, I am very lucky and yes, he is very handsome. But there's so much more to him than what he looks like. Nobody knows that except for me. And nobody will ever know because he is mine." But I stay silent.

Through the tears, I smile to myself. I know what I just told myself is true, and nobody can take him away from me.

Chapter Eight

At the age of thirty-one, I've achieved most of what I wanted to do with my life. I'm the CEO of my family's company, I have my own fortune, I possess every toy that any red-blooded American male worth his damn salt would desire: a private plane, a penthouse apartment in Manhattan, a car and loyal driver at my disposal 24/7. Basically, I fucking own this town.

But none of this is worth shit without her. Without Allegra.

I knew it was going to be tough not being able to see her at a moment's notice. I prepared myself for the torture. But it's worse than that.

I fucking *crave* her.

I crave the sound of her. Her sweet laugh that's genuine and infectious, easy on the ears, never rough or forced. Her voice when she sings, so pure and angelic, perfectly hitting the high notes that an opera demands. Her smart mouth full of wiseass remarks when she's admonishing me for something I've done that arouses me to the point of making my dick hard.

I crave the smell of her, especially her coconut shampoo, even though I could just pop open the bottle that's sitting in my shower. But it wouldn't be the same because it isn't on her gorgeous silky brown hair that I could raise to my nose, allowing it to intoxicate me.

I crave the feel of her. The way she feels sitting in my lap, how she fits perfectly when we lie next to each other, her soft curves folding into my chest and torso seamlessly so I could curl my arm around her.

I crave the taste of her. I miss being able to spread her smooth thighs so I can insert my tongue into her pussy, where she tastes like the purest honey.

Saying good-bye to her on my jet in Milan exactly a week ago today was excruciating. I tried to lighten the mood by giving her the whole *Hey, no big deal, there are phones, Skype, texts* speech. But she saw right through me, like she always does, playing along, trying to be strong for me, because she is—strong, courageous, brave, always putting others before herself. More selfless than I'll ever be.

So when I'm at my office, like I am now, I sit at the table instead of my desk because of the photo of her that rests there, tormenting me. I can't get any work done otherwise. I become fucking useless when I sit there because I can just stare at it for hours.

Papers and files are spread around me. I'm trying to analyze a spreadsheet of projected earnings, but it's just gibberish to me. I can't fucking focus.

The intercom buzzes. My secretary's voice comes over the speaker. "Sir, there's someone on the phone for you who says he's an associate of your father's and he says he needs to speak with you urgently, but he won't give me his name."

"That's all right, Eleanor. I'll take it."

I press the line that's lit. "This is Davison Berkeley."

"Tell your father to think twice," a rough voice whispers.

"Excuse me? Who is this?" I demand.

The other line goes *click*.

"What the hell?" I ask aloud, looking at the phone as if it could reply. I slam the receiver down into its cradle. Grabbing my jacket, I throw it on and head out the door.

"I'm going to see my father," I shout over my shoulder to Eleanor. I storm down the hallway to my father's corner office. I completely ignore his assistant's pleas to wait as I push through his door, finding him on the phone, his feet thrust up on his desk as he leans back into his leather desk chair.

"What the hell, Mal? Didn't you check them out first?" he's saying to someone.

He finally acknowledges my presence, glancing over and grimacing at the sight of me.

"Davison's here. I have to call you back," he informs whoever Mal is, sounding very annoyed.

He hangs up, then turns to me, looking bothered as usual when it concerns me, his own son.

"You ever heard of knocking?" he snaps at me.

I disregard his question because I have no time for his bullshit. This is distracting me from my own work. Like I fucking need this.

"Why would someone tell me to tell you to think twice?" I demand right back.

He stares at me passively, no sign of anxiety or recognition crossing his face. The problem is, that's his poker face, and I should know because I've mastered it myself thanks to genetics.

"How the hell should I know? And what are you talking about?"

"Someone just called my office telling me to pass on that message to you. Tell me what that person meant, Dad," I demand of him again, this time not hiding my impatience.

"I have no clue," he stresses, his eyes unwavering.

I take a deep breath and exhale, completely frustrated.

"There's nothing going on," he replies, rubbing the back of his neck with his right hand. And there it is. His tell. He's lying straight to my face.

My face starts to heat when I point my finger at him. "And *that* right there, Dad, is why I know something is going on with you!"

A thought hits me like a streak of goddamn lightning. Ian Parker. The Bulldog never got back to me about what he found.

"This isn't over," I warn him.

Without waiting for my father's reply, I thunder out of my father's office back down to mine. "Get Ian Parker in my office right now!" I order Eleanor as I slam my door behind me.

Within two minutes, I'm sitting behind my desk, with Ian standing on my carpet.

"Did you talk to Dominic about the mix-up on the quarterly report?" I ask him pointedly.

"Yes, sir. He said it was a mistake, but…"

Ian starts fidgeting, his eyes shifting down to the carpet.

"What? Spit it out," I demand.

He looks back up at me. "When I pointed out the discrepancy, he acted suspiciously. It was as if he was feigning surprise, like he was just pretending."

"You should've told me this right after you confronted him," I reprimand him.

"I know, sir," he replies sheepishly. "I was wrong not to do that. I'm very sorry."

I nod my head. "I appreciate that. Keep me informed if anything else develops."

"Yes, Mr. Berkeley."

Once he leaves, I sit back in my chair. I sigh in exasperation.

What the fuck is going on? Dominic is the key to all this. And he's going to give me a straight answer.

As I rise to my feet to go down to Dominic's office, the intercom buzzes with Eleanor's voice. "Sir, Charles is waiting downstairs."

I check my watch. *Fuck.* I need to head uptown for my business lunch at Le Cirque with a potential client.

As Charles speeds up the FDR along the East River, I pull out my cell to leave a message for Dominic. "Dominic, this is Davison. We need to speak as soon as possible. Be in my office at four o'clock. Don't be late."

Once I end the call, I remove my iPod from my jacket breast pocket. I connect it to the dock I had custom-installed in the Maybach after Allegra bought the player for me. Sade's smooth voice comes over the speakers, launching into the trifecta she downloaded for me, the one that she told me about when we said good-bye on the jet—"The Sweetest Taboo," "Kiss of Life," and the one that resonates with me the most, "Nothing Can Come Between Us." I imagine her sitting next to me, her intoxicating scent filling the car, her lilting voice raising my spirit, her gentle touch calming me, her soft lips on mine, kissing me gently at first, then becoming more insistent as our desire grows until the need to have my cock inside her drives me wild as she straddles my lap, taking me into her...

My head falls back on the headrest as I sigh in frustration.

Torture. Absolute, unmitigated fucking torture.

* * *

I check my watch. 4:15. My CFO is fifteen minutes late.

"Sir, Mr. Craig is here," Eleanor's voice announces over the intercom.

About fucking time.

"Send him in."

Dominic Craig, the CFO of Berkeley Holdings, walks his portly body through my office door, a smirk on his face.

"You summoned me?" he asks snidely, about to plant himself in a chair across from my desk.

The fucking balls on this jerk.

"Don't bother sitting down. And yes, I summoned you. I'm your fucking CEO, so check that attitude of yours right now."

I have to curb my impulse to laugh at the sight of his toupee, which is sitting on the top of his bald head, slightly askew. His suits are starting to fit snugly around his body.

He remains standing and takes a deep breath. "Fine. What's going on?"

"Something's come to my attention. There seems to be a mix-up of the numbers on the latest quarterly report," I tell him, watching his reaction. "Why would that be?"

"How the hell should I know?" he spits back at me.

"You should know because you're the goddamn CFO," I remind him.

"Who told you…" he starts. "Oh, wait, it was that lackey Ian Parker, wasn't it? Why did he report to you first?"

"Seeing as I'm the CEO of the company, I thought it would be glaringly obvious why he came to me first." I pause, then lean forward in my chair. "So, having said that, tell me, Dominic. Why *did* the confusion happen?"

"Human error, that's all," he replies dismissively.

"Right, but why did it take Ian coming to me and not you to bring this to my attention?"

A strange look comes over his face, almost as if he knows he's about to lie and has to believe the lie himself so I will in turn. "It slipped my mind."

I can tell instantly it's just a smoke screen. "I see."

"Anything else?" he asks impatiently.

"No, that's all."

I watch him walk out, and a gut feeling overtakes me. He was sussing me out. He wanted to see what I knew so he could report to someone else. And something tells me it's my father.

* * *

ALLEGRA

"No! No! No!"

La Diva's voice bounces off the high frescoed ceilings as it re-verberates throughout the opulent room in her villa that's used as a rehearsal space. Her trusted accompanist on the piano, an older woman named Leonora, suddenly stops playing.

I sigh, dropping my head to the floor.

What does this woman want from me?

I know I'm lucky, even blessed, to be where I am right now, training under La Diva. But at this moment, I'd give anything to be waking up next to Davison, feeling his arms around me, his hot breath on my neck, his deep voice rumbling in my ear, his cock—

"Allegra!"

The frustration in her voice rattles me.

"Focus! You are not singing Mimi! You are singing Musetta! She is outgoing. She likes to flirt. She is coquettish. She is *not* dying from tuberculosis!"

When I first arrived, La Diva and I worked on perfecting the role of Mimi in *La Bohème*, which we both decided would be the ideal signature role for me. But now, she wanted me to prac-tice singing the role of Musetta, a singer who has an on-and-off relationship with Marcello, a struggling poet, and when she first appears in Act II, she is dating Alcindoro, a wealthy, older man who buys her anything she wants. She has a famous aria that she sings to Marcello to try to get him back, known as "Musetta's Waltz." I'd always thought of her as the Ado Annie of opera, the character from *Oklahoma!* who strings along two men without a care in the world.

I swallow in my throat. "I don't know…*non lo so*…"

"*Che?* What?" she demands.

"I've never strung men along. I've never been outgoing. I—"

"*Basta!* Enough!" she shouts. "*Cara*, it's not just about the voice. You are singing, but you are also acting."

I look up, trying to keep the tears of exasperation from falling down my cheeks, my dampened eyes visible to my teacher. I watch as she walks over to Leonora, whispers in her ear, then comes over to me as the other woman leaves the room.

La Diva's warm, wrinkled hand clasps mine. "Come with me."

In a fiery red silk caftan with matching silk pants and high heels, La Diva leads me to an upholstered love seat in a far corner of the room and sits us both down.

"Allegra, I know that you have been through so much pain, and you can use that for Mimi."

I nod as she continues.

"But with Musetta, I can see that her character is not something you can relate to, or so you think."

"Exactly. I can't. It's not in my nature…" I ramble, gesturing with my hands as if I were trying to find the right words to explain myself.

She holds up her hand, her palm facing me. "Stop. Your *ragazzo*, Davison. He is very handsome."

"*Sì.*" I smile slightly at the thought of my love. "*Molto bello.*"

"How did you first meet?"

I grin widely as I recall that moment. "He came to the restaurant where I work to retrieve a glove he'd lost."

"And how did you feel when you first saw him? Talked to him?"

"I was very attracted to him. But it wasn't just because he's handsome. The second we started talking to each other, it was as if a match had been lit between us. A spark was ignited. I recognized something in him, something deep and soulful. And from that moment on, as much as I tried to ignore my feelings for him, I craved him."

"So you didn't have to, how do you say, string him along. And from what I could tell from our time together, he's probably made you more confident, more sure of yourself."

I nod in agreement, smiling. "Yes, you could definitely say that."

"*Bene.* Then use that confidence when you are Musetta. Yes, you and your *ragazzo* are together. *Insieme.* But surely there are times when you take the lead?"

I laugh nervously at her supposition, slightly taken aback. La Diva is known for her colorful history, so I shouldn't have been surprised.

"Yes, I have taken the lead at times, Signora," I admit.

She looks relieved, clamping a hand over her chest. "*Grazie!* From one Italian woman to another, you had me worried there for a moment."

I laugh at her reaction.

"So, knowing that, use that image when you sing Musetta. You are seducing Marcello, enchanting him." She glances at the gold watch on her wrist. "I think that's enough for this morning. Use your free time to practice. I'll see you later and we'll pick up where we left off."

La Diva rises to her feet and walks out, with a scented cloud of Shalimar remaining in the air. I let my head fall back onto my seat, closing my eyes and sighing aloud in exhaustion.

"She's called La Diva for a reason."

An American accent forces me to open my eyes, not just because I didn't see the man enter the room, but also for its familiarity, a voice I hadn't heard in three years.

When I raise my head, a tall, lean man is standing a few feet from me. My eyes widen, and my mouth drops in shock.

Matteo Garibaldi is standing in front of me.

Dressed in a white T-shirt, worn jeans, and soccer shoes, his straight black hair flops over his forehead, just like it did the entire time we dated on and off in college.

"Hello, Allegra," he says to me, his pale blue eyes boring into me.

"What the hell are you doing here?" I ask, my voice raspy after singing all morning.

A mischievous smile crosses his face. "La Diva is my aunt on my mom's side. I'm her assistant for the summer."

Mystery solved.

My ex-boyfriend is here for the entire month.

Fabulous.

Chapter Nine

The digital clock on my nightstand reads 5:01. I'm lying on my bed leaning back against the pillows in a pair of boxer shorts. My laptop is on and fully charged. Now I'm just waiting for Allegra's call. With the six-hour time difference between New York and Milan, I don't want her staying up at night waiting to reach me at a decent hour on my side of the Atlantic. So whenever we Skype, I leave my office at four thirty and have Charles drive me home to make it in time for her call at five.

A ringing sound starts beeping from my computer. I smile and click to answer her.

A few seconds pass…

There she is, my heart leaps out of my damn chest, and everything is fucking right in my world.

"Hey, baby."

Her eyes light up as she smiles back at me. As far as I can tell, the only thing she's got on is my Harvard sweatshirt, the one I always wear. Without telling me, she snagged it from my closet before she left for Italy. In its place, I found the other sweatshirt she always wears when she stays over at my apartment. It was sneaky of her, but it worked, because when I need to be close to her, I wear it, her delicious scent attached to it, which temporarily dissipates the torture of missing her.

"Hi," she says quietly. "How are you, Harvard?"

I smile back at her. "Better now that I can see your gorgeous face and hear your angelic voice. How was your day?"

"Long. La Diva kicked my ass today."

"More so than usual?"

"Yeah," she sighs. "I couldn't get into Musetta."

"From *La Bohème*?"

She shuts her eyes, nodding her head.

"What's going on, Venus?"

Her dark brown eyes open, softened and slightly moistened.

"I love that you know what opera Musetta is from and I didn't have to explain it to you."

"What can I say? My mother raised me right," I joke, trying to cheer her up.

It doesn't really work. She gives me a small smile and a nod, then looks away from the screen.

"Allegra, talk to me. What's wrong?"

Still not facing me, she sighs. "I just miss you like crazy, Davison. I miss waking up to your face and having breakfast with you. I miss having you pick me up after work, especially when we take the scenic route with stoplights."

I grin widely. "Venus, show me those beautiful brown eyes of yours."

She finally turns back to the screen to look at me. Her eyes are still wet and her mouth is downturned.

"I miss all of that too, especially the stoplights. I *really* miss them," I tell her, hoping like hell she'll smile back at me.

Yes!

A wicked grin crosses her face, and I'm rewarded with her eyes shining brightly back at me.

She leans closer to the computer and whispers, "So, tell me, then, Mr. Berkeley, what do you miss most? This?"

Before I have a chance to ask what she meant by that, she pulls off the sweatshirt, revealing her voluptuous tits, with their rose-colored nipples pointing back at me. My cock hardens instantly at the sight of them.

"Oh yeah, baby," I groan. "I miss those beauties a fucking ton."

"That's nice to hear," she purrs. Then she leans back, hooks her panties with her thumbs, and pulls them down. She spreads her legs wide-open, and I can see her pussy, wet and glistening in the light.

"Hang on, baby. Don't start without me," I ask of her as I lift myself to yank off my boxers.

When I look back at the screen, she's massaging the outer lips of her gorgeous cunt, fingering it with her right hand while kneading her left breast with the other.

"I miss you so much, Davison," she whispers.

My knees fall to the sides as I open my legs far enough so she can see me as I'm stroking my hard cock, watching as my exquisite girlfriend pleasures herself. "I know. Imagine that's me touching you, pinching your nipples, massaging your succulent tits. You look so fucking hot right now, baby."

She starts to moan as she plunges a finger into her pussy, looking for that sweet spot that makes her scream in ecstasy when I suckle it with my mouth.

"Open your eyes, Allegra."

She looks at me, her eyes hooded with arousal and desire.

"Do you see this?" I ask her as I continue pumping my cock. "This is all for you, my love. Right now, your lush mouth is sucking on it, nice and hard just the way I like it, your warm tongue swirling around the tip so softly."

I can see her fingers speeding up as they plunge over and over into her pussy, her breast clamped tightly in her other hand as she rolls the nipple between her fingers.

"I'm so close," she pants.

I speed up working my dick. "You are a sex goddess, baby. *My* sex goddess. God, I wish like fuck I could taste you right now."

We're now working at the same pace, anxious for our mutual release.

"Come for me now," I command her.

Her head falls back as she shouts my name at the top of her lungs, which pushes me to the edge as my orgasm shatters me, a white ribbon of cum spurting from the tip of my cock.

My head tilts up on my pillow, gasping for air. When I start breathing normally again, I sit up to see my beautiful love waiting for me with a huge smile on her face.

"That was amazing," she says in a sated, ethereal voice.

I reach over for the wet towel I always leave next to me to clean myself off. "I'd have to agree, Venus. After you took off my sweat-shirt—"

"*My* sweatshirt."

"We'll discuss ownership rights regarding my wardrobe when you return. What I was going to say was that I barely had enough strength to restrain myself from just getting on with it when I asked about your day. And then you took it off and I thought, *Thank fucking God.*" I laugh.

She laughs in return. "I know. And it's totally fine with me be-cause you made me smile, the first time I have all day. You have the golden touch, Harvard."

"I aim to please, Venus," I reply, smiling back at her.

"And you always do." She shifts back. "So, something weird happened today."

I continue wiping off my belly without looking up. "What?"

"My ex-boyfriend from college is here. Turns out La Diva is his aunt on his mom's side."

What the fuck?

I stop cleaning myself, looking up from my torso into the screen. "Run that by me again."

I can see her swallow in her throat. "It's no big deal, Davison. Apparently, Matteo works as her assistant for the summer."

"And you don't think it's a coincidence that he just happened to be there?"

"What are you talking about?"

"Come on, Allegra! Don't be so fucking naïve! She probably told her sister about you coming there, and she just happens to be his mother, and she passed that news on to him. And now I have to worry about him trying to get into your pants! Do you have any idea how much I'd rather it was me there with you than him? This is just great."

I watch as she throws on the sweatshirt, the mood now completely lost. "Christ, Davison! What do you take me for? Of course I have an idea about that, because I have the exact same one! I love *you*! And he's afraid of commitment. Remember I told you that?"

"Yeah, I remember, but it's been what? Three years since you last saw him? A lot can happen in that time."

"We're just friends," she sighs.

"You might believe that, but I seriously doubt that he does."

"Don't you trust me?" she demands, her eyes blazing with fury at me.

I can't believe this.

"Of course I trust you!" I snap at her. "It's him I don't trust."

"Well, right now, that's not exactly the vibe I'm getting from you, and it's pissing me off. So, thanks for ruining our night, Davison. I'll talk to you later."

Before I can stop her, she hangs up. When I call her back, she ignores me.

"Fuck!"

Great. Just fucking great. This is all I need.

I jump off the bed and head straight into the shower to try and calm myself down. As I wash off, I spot her coconut shampoo. I grab it and slam it to the floor, watching as the bottle pops open and the sweet-smelling fluid pours into the drain.

"Goddamn it!" I shout, my voice bouncing off the tiled walls.

I leave the bottle where it is when I finish, grabbing a towel and wrapping it around my waist. I storm into the bedroom and snatch my phone from my bed. I scroll through it in search of my pilot's number. I don't see it and hurl my phone across the room, landing with a *thud* on the carpet.

"Motherfucker!"

I drop to my bed, my heart pounding against my chest. I shut my eyes tightly and take a deep breath.

Trust her, you dick. She's got this. And she fucking loves you.

With a sigh, I stand up and pad into the kitchen. I reach for the bottle of Jameson in my liquor cabinet, filling a tumbler with three fingers' worth of the amber liquid. I bring the glass with me into the living room, where I collapse on the couch and let the whiskey course through my system, burning my throat, allowing it to dull my senses and deaden the pain of my love being so damn far away from me, with her ex-boyfriend under the same roof as her and undoubtedly prepared to take back what he lost all those years ago.

* * *

ALLEGRA

Staring into the bathroom mirror the next morning, a pair of bloodshot eyes and dark circles are looking back at me. I'm still wearing the Harvard sweatshirt I swiped from Davison's closet before I left, and my hair looks like a damn bird's nest.

I barely slept at all last night. I know Davison is worried about me, and he trusts me implicitly. I try to rationalize the reasons for him becoming upset last night, everything from telling him that my ex-boyfriend showed up unexpectedly to the glaring fact that he can't do anything about it. Basically, these things are out of his control, and it's driving him mad.

The more I think about it, all of those reasons can apply to me as well.

We're angry for the same reasons. And in some bizarre way, that brings me comfort.

For the first time since I hung up on him, I take a deep cleansing breath, reminding myself about my phone appointment with Dr. Turner later in the afternoon. We've arranged to keep our sessions going while I'm in Italy.

First, my ex-boyfriend shows up, then I have an argument with Davison about trust.

Dr. Turner is going to have a field day.

Before I can reach for my toothbrush, I hear someone knocking on the door of my suite.

When I open it, Matteo's tall form is standing in the doorway, dressed in a black V-neck T-shirt with the same jeans and shoes he was wearing yesterday when I first saw him.

Shit. I can't handle seeing anyone now, let alone my ex-boyfriend, who seems to have appeared out of nowhere.

"Morning," he says with a bit more enthusiasm than I would prefer after such a crap night. "Geez, you look like hell."

"I didn't sleep well," I tell him, not bothering to mask my displeasure at his comment.

"I thought we could have breakfast in the solarium this morning. You know, catch up before you have your morning session with my aunt."

At first, I want to decline his invitation, but knowing what I have to face this morning thanks to Matteo's reminder, I decide I need something in my stomach and a strong cup of cappuccino to wake me up.

"Sure. Just give me a minute."

I slip into my flip-flops and quickly brush my hair. Deciding I look decent in my sweatshirt and sweatpants, I open the door again to a smiling Matteo. He runs a hand through his long, dark hair. "Ready?"

I grunt in reply at his question, causing him to laugh out loud, which irritates the hell out of me.

We walk silently along the marble corridor to the solarium on the edge of the wing where La Diva's apprentices stay. Her entire villa is a vision of opulence from the materials that were used to build and furnish it, such as the Carrara marble and stained glass windows to the Persian carpets and Murano chandeliers. I wouldn't have expected anything less from a woman of her fame and fortune. Even after a week of being here, I'm still intimidated by the luxury of it all, and I doubt that feeling will pass.

The sun is shining brilliantly when I walk into the glassed-in space, wishing I'd brought my sunglasses to shield my eyes. The table I usually sit at by myself for breakfast is set for two today. The food warmers on a side table are already set up. This morning, I decide I need protein and carbs to fill me up, so I settle on scrambled eggs, buttered toast, a small glass of orange juice, and a steaming cup of cappuccino. Matteo settles on oatmeal with bananas, and we tuck into our food simultaneously.

Matteo is first to break the silence between us. "So…"

"What?"

"You sing opera now, huh?"

I roll my eyes, so not in the mood for playing catch-up this morning, my mind still on my argument with Davison. "That's stating the obvious. I wouldn't be here if I didn't."

"Wow. Sorry, just trying to make conversation," he says in apology.

I take a deep breath.

Suck it up. He's just trying to be nice.

"I'm sorry. Seeing you after so long came as a shock to me, and last night I had an argument with someone."

"No problem," he says with a slight smile. "How have you been? How's your father? Still running the butcher shop?"

"Yeah. I've been good. He still has the shop. I graduated from the Gotham Conservatory, and then thanks to my professor, your aunt offered me the apprenticeship. What about you?"

He swallows a spoonful of oatmeal before answering. "After we graduated, I couldn't decide on what I wanted to do with my life. I dabbled in a bunch of stuff, from being an assistant in an art gallery to working in a vintage record store. But in the fall, I'm going to Pratt in Brooklyn for a master's degree in digital arts."

"Oh, that sounds cool. How's your family?"

"Crazy as ever," he smiles. "We still live in Brooklyn."

"Near Coney Island?"

He smiles. "Yeah. Some of the best times I've ever had in my life were on the Cyclone with you when you held on to my hand so tight that it practically lost circulation."

I smile. "I remember. I was screaming at the top of my lungs."

"Blowing out my eardrum in the process."

Suddenly, a thought crosses my mind. "Wait, I'm curious. Why haven't I seen you since I've been here?"

"I was in Milan working on some business matters for my aunt. I've been going back and forth between here and the city."

As I take a sip of my coffee, something Davison mentioned when we were arguing last night pops into my head.

"So, do you work for your aunt every summer?"

"I did for a while after we graduated because my mom made me, mostly because she thought I needed something stable. I wasn't going to this summer since I told her I got into Pratt, but when she told me you were going to be Zia Ginevra's apprentice, I knew I couldn't say no to my aunt."

I shut my eyes and take a deep breath.

Damn it. Davison was right.

The feel of a warm, heavy hand on mine makes me snap my eyes open. "Hey, are you okay?" he asks, a worried look in his eyes.

"Yeah, I'm fine."

"Are you seeing anyone?"

The speed of his question after my reply takes me aback. I swiftly pull my hand away from his. "Wow. Blunt much?"

"Just curious," he replies casually, but the way his eyes are staring back at me, unwavering, waiting for my answer, he's dead serious.

"I am. We've been dating since November."

"What's he like?"

"Davison works for his family's company on Wall Street," I reply.

"Sounds rich."

"He does have money, but it's not why I'm with him. We just…fit, you know?" I smile as I think of my Harvard.

"Good. I'm glad." He runs a hand through his hair. "Would you like to have dinner tonight to catch up some more?"

I sigh. "Sure, that'd be fine."

"I'll come by around seven."

"Works for me." I glance at the small gold clock on the side table. "I'd better go get ready for my session. I'll see you tonight."

"Great. I look forward to it."

Once I'm dressed to meet La Diva, I sit down on my bed for a minute before I head out, shut my eyes, and think of my breakfast with Matteo and how different Davison is from him. Everything about Davison—his confidence, his constancy, his strength, and most of all, his devotion to me, makes me grateful for all of it, for all of him. And even if he would be upset knowing I'm having dinner with Matteo, nothing will happen with him because I love Davison. I smile recalling what I told Matteo because it's true. Davison and I just fit.

Chapter Ten

In the past twenty-one hours, I've learned more about my girl-friend than I knew before—Allegra Orsini really *is* the most stubborn woman I've ever known. I even used Google Translate to find out how to say that in Italian: *"La mia ragazza è la persona più testarda che ho conosciuto."*

She refuses to reply to any of my e-mails or texts, and my Skype calls are going straight to voice mail.

I'm past the point of being pissed off.

I'm fucking *livid*.

I glance at my watch, realizing it's past two o'clock and I totally forgot to eat lunch.

I'm working from home today because I can't deal with any bullshit from my executives. I need peace and quiet.

Suddenly, the security phone next to my elevator buzzes.

Spoke too soon.

I put my laptop aside and pad over to it.

The voice of the doorman on duty comes over the line. "Sir, Miss Canterbury is here to see you. She says it's urgent."

Fuck. What does she want now?

"It usually is." I sigh. "Fine, send her up."

A minute later, the *ding* of the elevator announces her arrival, as does the noxious perfume I always hated on her.

"What do you want, Ashton? I'm busy." I can't help but be terse with her. She doesn't deserve any better, really.

But now that I'm studying her more closely, I realize something's off. Her hair is pushed back with a headband, and she's wearing sweats. If I learned anything from dating her, it's that she never wears sweats in public, even if they are cashmere. And even more, her hands are trembling and she looks pale.

For as long as I've known her, I've never once seen her like this. Vulnerable and scared. She keeps clasping and unclasping her hands from what I can only assume is nervousness.

I take a deep breath to calm myself down. "Okay, what's wrong?"

"You know I wouldn't have come here if it weren't something important. It's just that…I got a strange phone call."

"About what?"

"Someone told me to tell my father to think twice."

Shit.

My pulse starts to quicken.

She takes a step closer to me. "You know something, don't you? I can tell from the look on your face."

My mind begins racing as I recall the phone conversation my father was having when I walked into his office. "I got the same phone call. Then I went to see my father about it, and I think he was on the phone with your dad, because I heard him say 'Mal.'"

"Malcolm…" she says, whispering her father's full name. "What do you think it means?"

"I don't know," I reply to her, shaking my head. "Did you ask him about it?"

"Yeah, and he completely evaded my question."

I take a breath. "Okay, if anything else happens, I want you to let me know."

"Do you think they're up to something?" she asks worriedly.

"I have no idea. But I'm going to find out." I hear the *beep* of an incoming text on my phone. "I should get that."

"Of course. Please keep me posted," she asks.

"I will."

She reaches for my arm, gripping it while looking at me sincerely. "Thank you, Davison."

I nod at her and watch as she steps into the elevator, the doors slamming firmly behind her.

I step back into the living room and reach for my cell phone on the coffee table.

I unlock the phone and read the text.

I purse my lips together, gritting my teeth. My fingers start flying over the screen.

I wait for the *beep* after I hear my father's voice telling me to leave a message.

"Dad, Ashton was just at my apartment and she's scared shitless over whatever it is you and Malcolm are involved in. You'd better straighten this shit out because it's not just threatening me but her as well, and probably the company, I'm guessing. Call me."

There. Done. Now I can get back to what really matters.

I search for the other number I need in my contacts list.

Once I hear the voice on the other end pick up, I start to issue instructions clearly and concisely so there are no fuckups. "Frank, fuel the jet and file a flight plan for Milan. I want to take off as soon as I get to Teterboro. I'll be there within the hour."

I rush into my bedroom and start throwing clothes into a duffel bag.

Enough of this bullshit. This ends now.

* * *

ALLEGRA

I love pasta. As much as I love eating it the way my father makes it back home, there's something about having it in Italy that makes it a religious experience. I don't know if it's the quality of the pasta or even the water used to boil it, but it tastes completely different here. When I eat it, I chew it slowly, reveling in the sublime taste of it in my mouth.

Pasta was the *primo piatto* at my dinner with Matteo in the solarium. For the *secondo piatto*, we had a fish course with a side dish of an *insalata*, and now, we're enjoying a dessert, or *dolce*, of chocolate gelato.

"Are you seeing anyone now?" I ask him.

"No. I just broke up with someone. She was getting too serious. I'm not at that point yet in my life where I'm ready to settle down."

"Hmm, sounds familiar," I tease him.

He rears back in surprise. "I thought I was doing the best thing for us."

I smile back at him. "I'm kidding. You were what I needed at the time. And it all worked out in the end because I'm with Davison now."

"Bet he doesn't try to cop a feel like we did when we made out on your couch while your father was downstairs in his shop."

I decide not to tell him about the time Davison finger-fucked me on that couch after he'd shown up at the shop to ask me to give him another chance.

"Umm…no, not at all," I tell him, pursing my lips together.

I take another bite of my heavenly dessert, seeing Matteo's eyes staring right back at me with an amused smile on his face.

"What?"

"You've got a spot of gelato on your chin."

"Oh…thanks," I murmur.

I start to wipe my chin as he keeps smiling and lets out a slight laugh. "No, you keep missing it. Here, let me," he offers.

As he starts to reach over with his hand to wipe it off, I lean away from his grasp and look away. "It's okay. I'll get it," I murmur.

When I glance back at him, a concerned look appears on his face. "Are you okay?"

Oh yeah, I'm peachy. I had a major fight with my overprotective boyfriend last night who's an entire ocean away from me, and you just tried to do something for me that I do for him on a regular basis because he can be a total slob when he eats.

I shake my head, giving him a slight smile. "Yeah, sorry. I'm just tired."

"No coffee for you, then?"

"Nope. I need to get some sleep tonight."

"Fair enough. Let me walk you back to your room."

We push away from the table, taking our plates, cutlery, and glasses over to the sideboard, piling everything neatly for La Diva's staff to collect later.

As we walk back to my room at the end of the wing, the only sounds in the cavernous hallway are our shoes against the marble floor. I'm finding it intimidating and oppressive, and I just want to get to my room and put on my pajamas and relax.

Matteo breaks the silence. "What are you singing tomorrow with my *zia*?"

"'Song to the Moon' from *Rusalka*."

"Have you sung in Czech before?"

"I have. It's difficult, but it's easier for me than German."

"I'm sure you'll be great," he reassures me.

When we arrive at my door, I unlock it and turn back to Matteo. "Thanks for dinner. I had a nice time."

Suddenly, he leans in closer to me, much too close for my liking. I put my hand on his chest and push him away, enough to make him wobble, forcing him to steady his footing against the marble floor.

"For the record, Matteo, you're too late," I inform him firmly without any hesitation, trying my best to hold back my disgust at him. "I have a boyfriend who I love and am devoted to, so we can only be friends. I hope that'll be enough for you. Now I want you to leave."

Matteo pauses for a second before replying. "Okay," he whispers.

He turns around, but stops once more to look back at me. "I'm really sorry. I wouldn't have hurt you, Allegra. I hope you know that," he offers to me in apology.

I give him a slight nod. "I do."

Taking two quick steps, I walk into my room and lock the door behind me, now safe and secure.

I quickly strip off my clothes, running to the bathroom to turn on the shower. As the hot water cascades down my back, I start to cry softly, missing Davison, reprimanding myself for yelling at him, refusing to believe that Matteo would try to take advantage of me.

Once I finish washing up, I crawl into bed and grab my cell phone. I check my texts and messages. Nothing from Davison.

I can't do this anymore. I was wrong, and he needs to know that.

Hearing his voice would shatter me, so I just decide on a text: *I'm sorry.*

I leave my phone on the rest of the night hoping I'll hear from him, praying for any form of communication at all. But when I wake up the next morning, I have an empty inbox.

It's too early to call him, but I will after my lesson, preparing to hear some form of *I told you so* coming from him. It's okay. I deserve it, and I can take it because I love him enough to admit it.

Chapter Eleven

The pebbles crunch under my driving shoes as I follow the curve of the path in the Signora's sumptuous garden. But I don't need directions, because within minutes of stepping foot outside, I hear Allegra. My Venus is calling me to her. I'm desperate for the sight of her.

She's singing something beautiful in a language I can't decipher, possibly Slavic. It's definitely something I've never heard her perform before. It sounds so sad, which makes me walk even faster to comfort her. I know it's probably just the tone of the aria itself, but after what we've gone through the past forty-eight hours, I'd hazard a guess that she's trying to extricate the pain she has to be feeling. She has to know that I was only upset because I love her and I wasn't with her to check this guy out and ensure that he wouldn't hurt her. I need her to believe me, to see it on my face in person, and I'm coming closer and closer to her with every step.

Finally, I reach a clearing where the path opens up to a view of the Lombardian hills, with my love standing with her back to me.

From where I stand, I can tell she's wearing a white cotton dress that billows softly in the wind around her legs, her sweet round ass filling it out. Her feet are bare, a pair of flip-flops lying casually on the side by a stone bench. That gorgeous silky brown hair of hers is pulled back in a ponytail. It's not going to be held together like that for much longer.

I watch her arms extend out, as if she's begging for something. Then she brings them together, her hands clasped together over her heart, her head down as she finishes the last note.

She takes a deep breath and turns to reach for something on the bench. She unscrews a water bottle to take a sip from it.

Finally, she turns and sees me.

The bottle falls to the ground, water spilling everywhere. Her right hand clamps over her mouth.

I take two steps toward her. My heart starts to race. My arms ache for her.

"Allegra…"

She doesn't say my name. She just runs to me, smiling widely through the tears streaming down her face.

I catch her in my arms as she jumps into them, her legs instantly coiling around my waist. I'm overcome from the pure joy of holding her again, her coconut scented hair intoxicating me, her heart beating just as fast as mine against my chest. Still crying, she wraps her arms around my neck, fisting my shirt in her hands.

"I'm here, baby, I'm here," I murmur, cradling her head with one hand and holding her curvy backside with the other.

I can hear her trying to catch her breath through her gulping sobs. "I'm sorry. I'm so sorry, Davison," she repeats over and over. She pulls her head back and sinks her tongue into my mouth. I can taste the salt from the tears on her lips. She's as ravenous for me as I am for her. I open my eyes and walk over to the bench and settle us onto it, her body still wrapped around me.

When we come up for air, she rests her forehead against mine. "I can't believe you're here," she manages to say.

"I am, baby," I tell her soothingly as I stroke her cheek.

"Davison…I just…I missed you so much," she starts to cry again.

"I know. It's been fucking torture for me. But I'm here now, so stop crying, okay?"

I hear a slight laugh from her. "Okay. But I just sang an aria about a water nymph wishing she could be human so she could be with her prince, so cut me some slack."

"Sounds kind of ironic, don't you think?"

She laughs out loud, and I just hold her even tighter. It's one thing to hear her laugh when we're on Skype with each other, but in person, it makes my damn heart soar.

"Your timing is impeccable as always, Harvard," she replies.

And hearing her call me that in person after being apart…it's fucking amazing.

She repositions herself more comfortably on my lap, which allows me to see her dress from the front. It has a halter top, which keeps her shoulders bare and accentuates her luscious breasts. I'm hard within seconds.

I reach out to tuck a strand of stray hair from her ponytail behind her ear. "Allegra, you have to know that I only got upset because I love you and I was worried about you."

"I do," she nods, leaning her head into mine. "It was just such a shock seeing Matteo here, and you were right."

"About which part?"

"He did come here knowing I would be."

My fists clench at her admission.

Motherfucker. I goddamn knew it.

"Look at me, baby," I tell her, gently yet firmly.

Her soft brown eyes stare into mine.

"Did he try anything?"

She shakes her head. "No."

I lift her chin so I can study her reaction more closely.

"Tell me again," I demand.

Her eyes lock on mine. "No, he didn't try anything."

I wonder if La Diva is offering acting lessons as well as singing lessons because her poker face seems to have disappeared.

Fuck this. I'll bring this up later because right now, I'm going to explode if I don't sink myself into her ASAP.

I put my hands on Allegra's waist and place her on the ground. I stand up, taking her face in my hands, and plant a short but deep kiss on her lips.

"That's it. We're getting out of here."

"What are you talking about?" she laughs.

Her smile makes me so damn happy. "You've been studying and singing about TB-ridden women and despondent lovers nonstop twenty-four/seven. You need a fucking break from them."

"That's my Davison," she purrs, her soft fingertips running over my cheeks, "always looking out for me."

"I'm serious," I insist.

She kisses me. "I know. I'm just teasing."

I moan in frustration.

"So, what are we doing?"

"I talked to the Signora, and she's letting you out of here for seventy-two hours."

"And where are we going?" she asks excitedly.

"It's a surprise. Just pack light."

"Why?"

"Because once we get to our destination, we'll be naked for most of our stay."

* * *

ALLEGRA

A few hours ago, I truly understood the meaning of several words: "grateful," "speechless," and "devoted" because those three words perfectly capture my state of mind when I saw Davison standing a few feet away from me on the Signora's garden path. The sight of him in his khakis and a tight black T-shirt that accentuated every muscle on his corded arms left me in such a condition where I couldn't form coherent sentences, and just so thankful that I could touch him and kiss him and tell him how sorry I was for acting like such a stubborn ass. And the fact that he flew all the way across the Atlantic to make sure I really *was* fine just proves to me how much he loves me and is always thinking of me.

Now, my head is lolled back on the butter-soft passenger seat of Davison's rental car—a sleek black Lamborghini, its engine roaring like a tiger when his lead foot hits the accelerator. I rolled my eyes when I stepped out of the villa and saw it sitting in La Diva's driveway.

Boys and their toys.

Wearing those dark aviator sunglasses that make him look so fucking hot, he's smoothly steering us along the curvy roads of the Lake Como region, or *Lago di Como* as it's known in Italian.

Soon, we're going to arrive at the lakeside villa that he has reserved for us for three days. He wasn't kidding when he said I wouldn't need much clothing because he actually supervised me as I quickly packed an overnight bag for our getaway—*Fuck yes!* for the retro-style red bikini and my jean shorts, and *No way in hell!* for the cotton pajamas and cardigan sweater, even though I argued that I might need the latter at night if it's a cool evening. He countered with, "I'm the only one who'll be keeping you warm, baby." I wasn't going to dispute that.

In between gear changes, Davison holds my hand, and when he has to shift, my hand remains on his right thigh, so both of us are always touching, knowing we're together in the same place and able to see and feel each other without thousands of miles and a computer screen separating us.

"We're here, Venus."

I look up to see a pebbled driveway situated between two stone pillars, a black metal gate protecting the property from intruders.

He swiftly jumps out of the car and pushes the gate open, hopping back in to drive us through, stopping to shut it, and then taking us down the hill. Tall, thin trees line the road as we follow it to the end, where my breath is taken away by the stunning view in front of me.

Dusk is setting over Lake Como, and lights are starting to pop up from the houses that sit on the water, each of them illuminating the azure water. The villa itself has three levels, painted in a cream palette, its window shutters contrasting against it in a darker, terra-cotta color. A small boat dock is sitting at the edge of the lake, where a classic wood-paneled speedboat is moored. As if this sumptuous home needed further gilding, an infinity pool looks out over the lake.

A pair of strong arms encircles my waist. "What do you think?" Davison whispers in my ear.

"It's beautiful, Davison. Thank you for bringing us here."

"My pleasure. Now we need to do something very important."

"What?"

"Pool sex," he declares, yanking me by the hand down the stone stairs.

"Harvard, it's freezing!" I counter.

"It's heated," he informs me.

In a split second, I let go of his hand and start pulling off my clothes, jumping into the water with a whoop of joy even before Davison manages to zip out of his pants.

* * *

As soon as Davison comes up for air from under the warm water, he yanks me to his strong, hard chest, slamming his mouth to mine. My ankles lock around Davison's torso. We start kissing each other fast and long and deep, desperate for the taste of each other that we've missed for far too long.

With our tongues tangled together, I sense him pulling me back toward the edge of the pool. He leans me against the side to support me as he searches for my pussy with one hand while holding me with the other. Once he finds it, he thrusts inside me as we both gasp aloud in sheer ecstasy. Finally, he is inside me. We are together.

The sounds surrounding us heighten my sensory overload, intensifying the euphoria of having his cock in me once more. Our moans and groans unite with the breezes that whisper through the leaves on the trees, a distant sound of a motorboat chugging past the villa on the lake, and the quacking of ducks standing on the shore. All of these nocturnal elements bring me to life again, increasing the heady sensation of being one with Davison.

Davison pants into my ear, "That's it, baby. Oh, fuck, you feel so good. God, I've missed you."

My head falls back, overwhelmed, enveloped in utter rapture. "Oh God…Davison, I need you so fucking much."

"I'm right here, Venus," he whispers roughly. "Not going anywhere. You're mine. All mine."

He leans in and tilts his head down so he can taste my nipples. I watch in pure awe as he laves each tip again and again, reveling in his passion. Then he clamps down hard on one, biting it, then licking it to soften the pain.

I gasp when he hits my clit with the tip of his glorious shaft, my arousal escalating with the heated water turning my blood into fire, coursing through every vein in my body. "Yes, Davison. Don't stop. I love when you fuck me so hard," I moan into his ear.

The water laps over the edge as Davison plunges into me over and over, forming a cascading waterfall. I grip his neck, my eyes staring up into the dark sky illuminated by a million stars.

"Fuck yes! Come for me, Allegra!" he shouts out in demand.

My entire body shudders as my orgasm overcomes me and I yell Davison's name in release.

As my core clamps down onto him like a vise, milking his swollen flesh, he follows my climax with his own, groaning like a roaring primal beast in heat, the veins in his neck straining against his flesh.

Our heads collapse onto each other's shoulders, with our breaths panting in tandem.

"Hi." His breath exhales softly onto my face.

"Hi."

He smiles. "I like my current position."

"Me too."

My fingers trace slow, soft circles on the nape of his neck, caressing his smooth flesh. We start to kiss again, slow and deep, moaning in pleasure, savoring each other.

When we stop, we're both grinning and sated. Something catches my attention above us. A line of statues is lit up by outdoor spotlights, standing along the wall above that separates the driveway from the second level where the pool is. Every statue is of a naked woman in a provocative pose.

"Got a question for you, Harvard."

"Shoot."

"Is there a reason there's a line of statues of naked women in various erotic positions up there?" I ask, gesturing with my nose toward them.

"Yes."

"And the reason would be?"

"The name of the villa is La Villa delle Donne."

"The Villa of Women," I translate into English. "Don't tell me the reason for that name is of a sexual nature."

"You'd be correct in that line of thinking," he admits. "A famous Italian playboy lived here once who was known for the exceptional penis that God endowed him with and the amount of ladies that it attracted, and they'd all end up here for orgies that lasted for days on end."

I pull back to look into his eyes. "Are you serious? Davison, I was joking! What did you do? Go on the Internet and enter 'luxury vacation homes with erotic histories for rent in the Italian Lake District' into a search engine like you did when we were in Venice?"

A wicked smile crosses his beautiful face. "I have my sources."

I roll my eyes. "Fine. Don't tell me. But wherever you did find this place, I'm grateful for it because this is heaven."

He leans in and kisses me deep and long. "Glad to hear it, baby," he rasps when we come up for air, touching his nose to mine. "Now we need to go eat so I have enough stamina to continue fucking you."

I grin back at him and without hesitation, I quickly disentangle myself from his arms and jump out of the pool, with Davison close behind.

Chapter Twelve

DAVISON

At this moment, I don't care what the fuck else is going on back in New York, because the only thing that matters to me right now is getting as many shots as I can of Allegra sitting on the stern of the vintage wood-paneled motorboat that comes with the villa. She's wearing the '50s retro-style red bikini I love that she wore when we were in Positano. The bright sun is beaming off her black Jackie O sunglasses, with the light highlighting her newly tanned skin from just a few hours on the boat. She is smiling widely as she looks out across the water, resembling an Italian sex goddess, which makes my cock hard.

My phone is on vibrate so she doesn't hear my phone clicking every time I take a picture of her. I know she'd be embarrassed and make me stop if she heard me doing it. But I wouldn't stop, because right now, the only thing that matters to me is recording every second of this moment. And anyway, I know she'd look damn hot shouting at me to put my phone away, so it's a win-win for me either way.

We took a tour around the lake, stopping at certain points when some of the villas that lined the shore took our breaths away, making us pause just to take in the magnificence of the private homes that have probably sat there for decades. Now we're sitting in a quiet spot by our villa, basking in the beauty of the summer day on Lake Como.

She turns to me, and I manage to quickly put my phone aside so she won't see it.

"Are you going to come up here any time soon?"

Just as I make a move toward her, she rises to her feet, flings her sunglasses to me, and gracefully dives into the sparkling blue water.

"Hey!" I shout.

Within seconds, she emerges from the waves, head bobbing, her silky cocoa-brown hair slicked back. "It was hot up there, Harvard. Maybe you should come and join me? It's so…nice…and…cool," she purrs, leaning back so her luscious tits tilt out from under the water, beckoning to me like a Muse out of *The Odyssey*.

"Don't have to ask me twice," I reply, putting her on notice.

I set her glasses on the leather seat, step up from the open cabin, and cannonball right into the water. I can hear her shouting, "You are such an ass, Berkeley!"

When I come up for air, a wave of water hits me smack in the face. "Jerk!"

"Watch it, baby," I warn her.

"Bring it, Money Boy!"

Yeah. She just did that. She just called me by Luciana's nickname for me.

"You asked for it, Orsini!" I warn her.

Before I know it, we are engaged in an all-out splash war. With each splash, I inch my way closer and closer to her.

"Get away, Davison! I'm still mad," she informs me, though the tone of her voice is more playful than angry.

The force of her splashes begins to die out. When I finally reach her, she murmurs, "I said, get away from me."

I smirk at her. Her eyes are blazing at me, not in fury, but desire.

She stays silent, our eyes fixed on each other as I reach around her and start to unhook her bikini top, which is not easy to do as I tread water. Once it comes away, I hurl the fabric up onto the boat, then wrap my arms around her.

Allegra links her arms around my neck and presses her tits into my chest.

I smile at her. "So I'm guessing I'm forgiven."

"You're quick, Harvard."

She curls her legs around my waist, grasps the back of my head, and starts to kiss me long and deep. With one hand holding her back, I slide the other into her bikini bottom, searching for her pussy.

Allegra whimpers into my mouth audibly, and I know what that means by now with my goddess. She's begging me not to stop.

I plunge my fingers into her wet cleft, working that sweet cunt of hers. When I brush across her clit, I rub it between the pads of my fingers as firmly as I can.

Allegra rips her mouth from mine, tilting her head back, pleading at the top of her lungs. "Fuck! Davison…"

Her soft body bucks against my torso. I watch in pure awe as her orgasm overcomes her, glorious in her release. I clamp my mouth on one of her tits, sucking it hard, prolonging the ecstasy for my Venus.

Her body shudders again. I smile as I listen to her moan, slowly returning her attention to me.

"You just finger fucked me in Lago di Como, Davison."

"I know. I was there," I smirk.

She kisses me quickly but softly. "Smart-ass. And now we should get back on the boat so we can fuck with you on top of me."

"My goodness. Such naughty words coming from my goddess's mouth."

"Your point being?" she asks with an upturned eyebrow.

"Get your lovely ass into that boat, baby. We'll fuck, and then we'll have a late lunch in Switzerland."

She smiles at me wickedly. "Hoist me up, Berkeley," she orders.

I shake my head, smirking at the sound of her bossiness that I love so much. "At your service, Venus."

* * *

The robust taste of my morning espresso gives me the jolt I need the next morning. Sitting in a chair on the balcony of our bedroom and wearing nothing but my boxers, I watch boats of various sizes pass by the villa on the lake. The sun beams down onto my chest, heating my skin.

I reach for my cell on the small bistro table and start to scroll through the pictures I took over the past seventy-two hours, mostly all of Allegra, with a few selfies of the both of us. The latest ones are from our day in Lugano. We spent the day sightseeing, eating, and shopping, ending it with a private boat tour of Lake Lugano, when I snapped a shot of her staring out at the water, a slight breeze lifting her hair, with a huge grin on her face. Everything I've done to get here, to see her that happy, is worth every penny I spent.

I also check my messages, and aside from a few e-mails from Eleanor at the office, there's nothing I can't handle from my current location. She reports that I haven't received any strange calls, and there was no word from Ashton, so hopefully nothing will change between now and my return to Manhattan later today.

I check the time and realize I need to wake Allegra so we can pack up and get the villa in order before we drive back to Milan.

Stepping into the bedroom, my eyes take in the exquisite body of the woman in the king-sized canopied bed, lying on her back. The white cotton flat sheet covers her torso, but her sumptuous breasts are bared for me to see with their dusty-rose-colored nipples, making me hard at the exposed view of them.

I take a deep breath, reminding myself that as much as I hate it, I need to get her moving.

I sit down on the bed next to her and slowly start to run my fingertips along her breasts, ending as I circle the areolas. I can see goose bumps popping up along her skin as she starts to shiver, jerking her awake.

"Morning, baby," I whisper.

"What time is it?" she mumbles.

"It's almost ten."

"Wonderful. I'm going back to sleep," she announces as she pulls up the sheet to cover herself, turning on her side facing away from me.

I yank it back down. "Allegra, I have to get you back to La Diva's today."

"Tell her I changed my mind. I want to be a rock singer instead. I'm going to be the next Joan Jett," she mutters, pulling the covers over her head.

I laugh at the image of her dressed in a red leather jumpsuit with an electric guitar strapped to her chest.

On the other hand...

I shake my head to get rid of the picture in my mind. Suddenly, I hear her start to sing the opening lines to "Bad Reputation," muffled by the cotton fabric. I laugh to myself, struggling to focus.

"Yeah, right. As if you could ever pull that song off," I remark dismissively.

"I can too," she insists. "I'm hurt that you doubt my singing skills, Harvard."

"Never. It's just the lyrics that don't suit your personality," I reply to placate her. "Maybe 'I Love Rock 'n' Roll' or 'Crimson and Clover.' Now, that I'd pay good money to see."

"I'll keep that in mind for future reference," she mumbles.

I sigh, tugging the sheet off her completely and pulling her off the bed. "Come on, woman! Let's go!" I order her.

"What the hell?" she shouts back at me.

I scoop her up into my arms and carry her into the master bathroom, with her squirming and protesting the entire way. "Stop it, Davison! Put me down!" she shouts.

I finally reach the shower, setting her down and turning it on before she can get away from me.

As the hot water falls over us, she starts splashing me with it. "You are such a jerk, Berkeley!"

I counter with my own offensive, grabbing the handheld shower head and aiming it right at her. She puts her hands over her face, trying to shield herself from the onslaught of the water.

"Wow, you can dish it out, but you sure can't take it, Orsini." I laugh.

"Okay, okay, I give! Stop it, Davison!" she pleads.

Instead of placing the shower head back in its cradle, I tilt it upward into the apex of her legs. I watch in fascination as her eyes widen in shock, but then she silently steps back to lean against the wall, spreading her legs and smiling teasingly at me.

I step toward her and resume my position, but then she clamps her hand over mine and directs the water into her pussy, hitting her clit at the perfect angle because the next thing I know, her eyes are rolling back with her head as she moans, "That's it, Davison. Right fucking there."

My cock is growing by the second as I see her arousal overcome her. I lean in to suck her breasts to heighten her excitement, slowly circling each nipple, letting it bob on the edge of my tongue.

"Kiss me," she whispers as she pulls me to her, forcing me to drop the shower head and kick it behind me. She plunges her tongue into my mouth as I grab her by the nape of her neck, devouring her. Her nails dig into my back, the spray of the water soothing their bite in my skin.

I can't stand it anymore. I have to be inside her.

I turn her around so her gorgeous ass is facing me. She instantly knows what I need from her. She widens her legs and pushes her hands into the wall so her backside is sticking up and out. I feel for the opening of her pussy, and when I find it, I shove my dick into her, listening to her gasp, "Ah…" in a mix of surprise and contentment.

With one word, my shaft swells to a thickness that fills her up. I begin to thrust into her, the sounds of flesh slapping against flesh and our moans bouncing off the three tiled walls and sheet of glass.

"Mine, Allegra. Never forget that. You. Are. Mine," I grunt, pounding into her harder and harder to emphasize each word so she remembers when I'm away from her.

"Never, Davison," she shouts to the ceiling. "I am yours."

Our bodies and groans unite, climaxing and shuddering simultaneously as I come into her. Her arms fall from the wall as she spins to me, yanking me to her, planting a deep kiss on my mouth.

She pulls back and smiles widely at me. "*Now* we can leave, Harvard."

* * *

I stare at the tall, lanky kid standing in front of me, because that's what he is. A kid.

Are you fucking kidding me?

This is the guy who she dated on and off for four years?

He's a total slacker. Dark hair that falls into his face like a sheepdog, jeans, and Chucks on his feet. And he's being too friendly with my girlfriend, making me more agitated by the second.

This guy, Matteo, just happened to be in the foyer of La Diva's home when we arrived after our drive from Lake Como, which I thought was a little too convenient. He has a messenger bag slung over his shoulder, heading out somewhere by the looks of it.

"Hey, Allegra," he greets her in a familiar tone that sets my blood boiling.

"Hi, Matteo," she replies quietly.

"Glad you're back." He smiles at her, to my disgust. "Did you have a nice time?"

"Very," she answers, gripping my hand tighter. "This is my boyfriend, Davison Berkeley."

That's right, asshole. Boyfriend. Her boyfriend.

Slacker runs his hand through his hair nervously before stretching it out to me in greeting. "Hi. It's nice to meet you. I've heard a lot about you."

Good. As well you should have. So hopefully that means you won't make a move on my girlfriend.

"We had a relaxing break in Lago di Como. Lots of eating, drinking, and *rest*," I happily inform him. "But it won't be long until she's back in New York and moving in with me."

In other words—hands off, Mr. Hipster.

Suddenly, my hand is being tightened in Allegra's grip, threatening my circulation. I know I just pissed her off, but I don't care. I'm staking my damn claim.

He looks surprised. "Oh, that's nice. Congratulations."

"Thank you," I tell him with as much civility as I can muster.

"Well...umm...I'd better get going. I need to run some errands for my aunt," he stammers. "It was nice to meet you, Mr. Berkeley. I'll see you later, Allegra."

"See you, Matteo," she calls after him.

"Great to meet you," I add on.

Once he's out of sight, Allegra turns to me. "What the hell was that, Davison? I'm not moving in with you—not any time soon, anyway."

"You're my girlfriend, Allegra!" I snap back at her. "It was a warning to him not to touch you."

"We're just friends. And I can take care of myself. Surely you know that by now?"

I sigh, taking a deep breath. "Yes, baby, of course I do. But I worry when I'm not with you, especially when you're so far away."

She cups my face with her soft hands. "It's just another seven days, Harvard. I'll be home before you know it."

"Might as well be ninety-seven days. It's still too long as far as I'm concerned. But I'm so proud that you're here and learning so much."

"I am, and that's the only reason I'm here and away from you," she reassures me.

"I know." I check my watch. "I hate to do this, but I'd better go."

"Okay," she whispers, dropping her hands to wrap her arms around me. "I can't tell you how much the past three days have meant to me."

My heart starts melting when I hear the catch in her voice. "I know how much, because they meant the same to me."

I pull back and kiss her, deep and long. Her mouth is warm, her tongue twisting with mine. When I hear her moan, I harden, but I know I have to stop or I'll never be able to leave.

We stop and stare at each other, no words necessary, except for three, which I say to her first.

"I love you."

"I love you too, Davison," she says, leaning her forehead on mine.

We stay like that for a few more minutes, then I plant one last kiss on her lips and turn for the door. Before I climb into the Lamborghini, I look back at her standing on the front steps. I give her a wave and blow her a kiss, which she reciprocates.

I gun the engine as I head down the long driveway, my hands wearing the driving gloves that brought Allegra and me together. I take a deep breath.

Seven more days. Just seven more fucking days.

* * *

ALLEGRA

"Alli!"

I hear Lucy's voice booming down the hallway in my apartment. The contents of my suitcase are strewn all over my bed as I'm unpacking, having arrived only two hours ago.

"In here!"

Within seconds, she appears in the doorway. "Hey, stranger! Welcome home!" she shouts, giving me a tight hug.

"Thanks. I've got some amaretto cookies and Perugina chocolates for you somewhere in this mess," I inform her, gesturing to my bed.

"No worries. So, all in all, is La Diva everything I've heard she is?"

"And then some. She gave me the courage to apply for the Metropolitan Opera National Council Auditions."

Her eyes widen. "You totally should. With your apprenticeship on your résumé and your incredible voice, you'd be a shoo-in to make it all the way to the finals. Could you imagine if you actually won one of the spots? It would totally launch your career."

"You should apply with me so we could go through it together," I suggest, hoping she will so I don't have to go through the audition process alone.

She shakes her head. "Nah. Too soon. I'm having too much fun with Tomas at the moment. Maybe I'll take a year off and just travel or something. He's been talking about taking me back to Prague to meet his family."

I rear back in surprise. "Wow, that's huge. Are you ready for that?"

"Why do you think I'm making him teach me Czech every chance I get? I already know the important words, like how to say 'harder,' 'faster,' 'suck'…"

I hold up my hand, palm facing out to her. "Okay, got it, thanks."

"So, how did you end things with Matteo?"

While I was in Italy, I'd e-mailed Lucy about him being there and the pass he made at me.

"I told him we could be friends, but nothing more than that. He gave me his phone number and e-mail address, but I didn't give him mine."

"Good move," she replies.

"I know. Davison got all territorial and possessive the second they met."

"Wish I could've been a fly on the wall for that. But you know he only acts like that because he loves you."

I sigh. "I know. And as annoying as it can be, I do love it," I admit.

Lucy glances at the clock on my nightstand. "Shit, I have to run. I'm meeting Tomas for lunch in Queens. He's giving me an introduction to Czech cuisine. So just give me my cookies and chocolates and nobody will get hurt."

I laugh aloud as I rummage through the souvenirs, finally handing Lucy her gifts.

She gives me a quick hug and kiss on the cheek. "Thanks, sweetie. When you want to start practicing for the auditions, let me know."

"Will do. Now go learn some Czech other than *Don't stop*."

"*Nepřestávej*," she shouts over her shoulder as she walks out.

* * *

The next night, I'm back at work. Le Bistro is busy as ever, especially now that it's summer and the outdoor seating area is open. The staff greeted me warmly when I walked in, and I quickly got back into the swing of things.

A well-dressed man in a blue suit who looks to be in his forties approaches me at the coat-check door. "Forgive me, but I think I might've misplaced my wallet. You wouldn't have happened to find it, would you?" he asks politely.

"Let me check, sir. This is my first night back."

I pull down the Lost and Found shoe box, but no wallet is inside.

"I'm sorry, sir. I didn't find anything," I report back to him when I return.

"That's all right. By the way, how's your boyfriend?"

My defenses immediately go up, and I go into protective mode. "Sir?"

"Davison Berkeley. I saw you once in the *Post* with him. And his father, Hartwell. He's doing well, I hope?"

"They're both fine, thank you." Chills start running up and down my arms. Something's up with this guy. "If you don't mind, it's my first night back, like I said, and I need to organize the space."

He gives me a small grin. "Certainly. Have a good evening."

I watch him exit the restaurant, and through the huge window that looks out onto the street, I see him get into a cab.

If he didn't have his wallet, he couldn't take a cab.

I step to the back of the room and grab my phone. Davison picks up on one ring.

His deep voice rumbles into my ear, instantly warming me all over. "Hey, baby."

"Hi. Listen, something odd just happened."

"What?" I can hear the worry in his voice.

"Some guy just asked me about you and your father."

His voice rises an octave. "What exactly did he say?"

"He wanted to know how both of you were doing. That's it."

"I'm coming over," he replies firmly.

"Why? It's only ten o'clock. We're not closing for another two hours."

"I'll be there in twenty minutes. And if anyone else talks to you about me or my dad, tell me immediately. Do you understand, Allegra?" he demands.

"Of course I do, but—"

The sound of his phone hanging up clicks in my ear.

What the hell was that?

Chapter Thirteen

DAVISON

Last night, when Allegra told me about that man asking her about my father and me, my blood ran cold, and I gripped my cell so hard that I could've crushed it with my bare hands. I cut her off and called Charles to bring the Maybach around to get to Le Bistro ASAP. I wasn't taking any chances. I managed to evade all of her questions on the way back to my place, and hopefully she'll stop asking them because I want to keep her safe from whatever is going on with my father.

Which is why I'm rushing down the hallway again at Berkeley Holdings this morning, ignoring the pleas of my father's assistant, and bursting through the doors of his office.

"I thought we went over this, Davison," he remarks without looking up from his copy of *Fortune*. "Knocking before entering is preferred."

I can barely contain my fury. "Look at me, Dad."

"I won't if you continue to use that tone with me," he replies in a cool demeanor.

"It's about Allegra."

The mention of her name finally prompts him to steal his focus away from his magazine. He gives me an annoyed look. "What about her?"

"Someone approached her at work last night asking about you and me."

He shrugs his shoulders. "So? It's not a secret you two are dating, much to my chagrin, and that you're my son. No big deal."

He starts reading the magazine again, causing me to grit my teeth and clench my fists.

I slam my hand down on the page he's reading to make sure he's paying attention.

He jumps back in shock. "Davison! What the hell is your problem?" he yells.

With my jaw clenched, I spit out at him, "Let me be perfectly clear with you. It's one thing to mess with me, but Allegra is off-limits. I don't know what you're involved in, but what you need to know is that there is nothing I won't do to protect her."

"You have nothing to worry about. It's being handled," he practically hisses back at me.

"And yet you won't tell me what exactly 'it' is."

"Because it's none of your fucking business, Davison. Now if you wouldn't mind, I'm busy."

I realize asking him anything more is pointless. I turn on my heel and head for the door, but look back at him before I leave. "Just know this, Dad. I'm not letting this slide. If whatever it is involves the company, I'm going to find out, one way or another."

I slam the door behind me, cursing my father all the way back to my office. I walk in and pull down the binder with the quarterly reports of the last twelve months from my bookshelf.

One way or another.

* * *

When I walk into my apartment around ten o'clock that night, I see abandoned floor cushions and candles sitting on my coffee table that are usually in my dining room. I check the refrigerator and see plastic containers of spaghetti and meatballs that weren't there this morning when I left for work.

Damn it. She must've wanted to surprise me. I am such an asshole.

I tug on my tie as I head for the bedroom, stopping in the doorway when I see Allegra's sexy naked form lying under my bedsheets, her sweet, luscious breasts poking out from under the cotton fabric.

I strip out of my suit, leaving everything on the floor and crawl into bed, joining her under the covers. I gently stroke her hair, stirring her awake.

"Davison? Is that you?" she murmurs.

"Hope you weren't expecting someone else," I joke.

She turns over to face me, immediately snuggling into my chest. "Why are you so late? What time is it?"

"Sorry, baby. It's about ten. Did you want to surprise me?"

"Yeah. Wanted to do something nice for you. The doorman let me in since I'm on your approved visitor list."

I really am such a shit.

"You're at the top of it, Venus. Permanently."

She tilts her head up so she can look into my eyes. She smiles slightly before a concerned look crosses her face. "Is everything okay?"

"Yes," I reassure her. "Everything is perfect." And it was. I was with her and that was all that mattered now. Thank God for the darkness, though, hiding from Allegra the worry etched on my face. The woman can read me like a book.

"You know, since you missed dinner, I think you deserve some dessert."

Before I can stop her, she disappears under the sheet and spreads my legs open.

"Hey, you don't have to—"

The feel of her warm tongue on the tip of my dick licking it like a lollipop instantly shuts me up. I fall back on my pillow, sighing from the pleasure she's giving me. My Venus is the most selfless woman I've ever known.

I grow harder with each touch of her hot tongue, laving along its sides, cradling and rubbing my heavy sack gently.

Then she grips the base of it as she starts sucking on it, bobbing up and down. I reach under the fabric and run my right hand through her silky hair, moaning in sheer pleasure from what she's doing with that skilled mouth of hers. "So good, baby. You are so fucking amazing."

Her speed increases, and I'm about to explode into her mouth. I roar as hot spurts flow into her mouth, my heart beating like a fucking jackrabbit's.

When she appears from under the covers, her face is flushed, bits of her hair sticking to her forehead. I take my thumb and wipe off her mouth.

"Come here, Venus."

She settles onto my chest, our pulses matching each other's beat for beat.

"I worry about you, Davison," she whispers.

I don't like the sound of that. "Why, baby?"

"You've just seemed preoccupied lately. Like you're not telling me something. You know you can tell me anything."

Her concern makes my heart soar. I swallow in my throat and answer her lightly, "It's nothing. Honestly. It's just been insane lately, you know, ruling the universe and all."

I sense her burrowing farther into my arms, which hopefully means she won't ask any more questions. I won't have my father's problems harming her in any way.

I lift her chin with my index finger so I can see her beautiful brown eyes. "Kiss me."

Our tastes mingle as my tongue tangles with hers. We kiss long and deep until I stop so I can tell her something.

"I promise you, Allegra. Nobody will ever hurt you again. You are mine and there's nothing I won't do to protect you."

Her eyebrows furrow in concern, but she doesn't say anything except, "I love you, Davison."

"As I love you," I tell her, cupping her face with my hands.

She leans into my touch, kissing one of my palms and settles on my chest. I hear her deep breaths as she falls back asleep.

I realize I just told her what I told my father about protecting her.

And it's true. There's nothing I won't do to keep her safe. *Nothing.*

* * *

ALLEGRA

I'm rubbing my eyes open the next morning as I'm walking toward the kitchen when something grabs my attention from the living room.

A baby grand piano is standing in one corner of the wide space, its black color glistening in the sunlight streaming through the windows.

"You like it?"

Davison's voice beckons from the kitchen entryway.

"It's amazing. When did it get here?"

"Early this morning."

I step toward it, running my hand over the smooth wood. I sense Davison's chest against my back.

"It's for you," he whispers.

I spin around to face him, my mouth dropped in shock.

"What do you mean?"

He smiles. "What part of *It's for you* did you not understand, Venus?"

"Explain, Harvard," she demands pointedly.

"You're probably going to be practicing now to enter some competitions, right?"

I nod.

"Well, in order to spend more time together, I figured you could practice here too, as well as at your house."

I cup his face with my hands, running them over his smooth skin. "You are too much, you know that?"

He grins at me like the damn cat that devoured the poor canary. "I know."

I bring his head closer to me so I can give him a long, wet kiss. "Thank you, Davison."

"You're welcome, baby."

I stare down at the shining piano keys, begging to be played. "Can I ask you something? And I want a straight answer."

"Of course," he quickly acquiesces.

"I know you have far more to handle at work than I could ever imagine, but you've never let it get to you the way it has been lately. Is there something more serious going on? Maybe I can help you in some way…"

As I'm saying all this to him, his jaw visibly clenches and his eyes grow serious. I know without a doubt that he's keeping something from me.

"It's nothing to worry about, Allegra. It's under control. And you do help me. Every moment you're with me, I know everything is right with the world." But even as he says this, worry etches into the lines of his forehead.

I take a deep breath, doing my best to keep myself calm and collected. "Damn it, Davison. I wish you would tell me. You know you can tell me anything."

He grabs me and envelops me in his arms, not saying a word. His grip on me is tight as I wrap my arms around him.

"Just remember I love you," I whisper to him.

He burrows his head into my neck. "I know."

We remain like that for a few minutes until he pulls back. "I have to get ready," he says, kissing me softly on the lips before turning for the bedroom, leaving me standing by the new piano alone.

I'm not keeping a scorecard of how many times we say those three words to each other, but he usually reciprocates when I say it first.

Could he be…

No. Impossible. Of course it is.

Isn't it?

Chapter Fourteen

DAVISON

Two days later, I'm back at my desk at Berkeley Holdings trying to focus on work, which I'm finding futile thanks to my frustration with my father, Dominic, and whatever the fuck is going on with them.

My desk phone rings, which means Eleanor must've stepped away momentarily.

"Davison Berkeley," I answer firmly.

"Mr. Berkeley, your father is playing a dangerous game," a deep male voice says on the other end. It sounds like the man who called me before. I grip the phone to keep my cool and decide to play along.

"Why don't you tell me about it?"

"I see your father isn't very forthcoming with you if you're asking me that question. And he should be if he knows what's good for him."

"Look, I'm sick of playing this game with you. You have no idea who you're messing with."

"I hope Allegra is doing well. She looked lovely when I spoke to her at Le Bistro."

WHAT THE FUCK?!?!

Holy shit.

It's the bastard who asked her about us that night.

"Listen to me, you asshole—"

He hangs up before I can finish.

I grab my cell and send my fingers flying over the screen.

Her name comes up and I press the number.

One ring…two rings…

"Goddamn it, Allegra! PICK UP!"

* * *

ALLEGRA

As Lucy plays Davison's baby grand, I use the view from his apartment as a focus point, singing "Song to the Moon" from *Rusalka*, which I worked on with La Diva. Tomas is here as well because I need his feedback on my Czech pronunciation.

Lucy brings the aria to a close in time with me as I sing the last line.

"God, this is a beautiful instrument," she comments on the piano. "And yours isn't bad either, Alli."

I roll my eyes at her. "Ha-ha. What did you think?"

"I guess just always remember what the aria is about—asking the moon to tell the prince that she loves him."

"I will. Tomas, what about my Czech?"

He doesn't reply right away.

"Yo, Prague Boy, how was her Czech?" Lucy snaps at him, trying to shake him out of his stupor.

Prague Boy. She has a nickname for everyone.

Tomas shakes his head. "Oh, it was fine."

Lucy and I look at each other, then back at him. "'Fine'? What kind of fucking critique is that?" Lucy shouts at her boyfriend. "Were you even paying attention?"

He jumps from his chair. "Luciana, stop…what is the word…nagging me!" he yells back at her.

We watch as he takes off for the bathroom. Lucy leaps from the piano bench and follows him. A door slams and I can hear shouting from behind it all the way from where I'm standing in the living room.

I sink to the piano bench, stunned at Tomas's sudden outburst. I instantly begin to feel awkward, wishing I were somewhere else.

My cell starts to vibrate on the coffee table. I turned off the ringer before we began rehearsing.

When I step over to pick it up, Davison's face is on the screen. "Hey, Harvard."

"Where are you right now?" he demands from me.

I'm not crazy about his rather impatient tone. "Davison, what's wrong?"

"Damn it! Answer me, Allegra!"

What the hell is with him?

"Will you stop yelling at me for crying out loud! I'm at your place."

"Doing what?"

"Practicing with Lucy and Tomas. Here, listen."

I put the phone on speaker before setting it on the piano and running my fingers over the ivory keys.

Once I finish, I grab the phone again. "There! Are you satisfied, Mr. Berkeley?"

He'd better be.

I hear him take a deep breath before answering me. "Yes."

"Good. I hope you won't be bringing that attitude home with you tonight. Otherwise, I'm not going to stay," I inform him.

"I won't. I promise," he whispers.

He hangs up before I have a chance to say good-bye.

As I stare at my phone attempting to comprehend what the hell just happened, Lucy comes back into the living room, her face red and jaw clenched. "Jerk."

I grow concerned at her appearance. "What happened?"

"Beats the shit out of me. He won't tell me what's going on with him no matter how much I try."

My mouth drops in surprise. "Same with Davison. He just called me to find out where I was and who I was with. He was totally checking up on me. And something's been up with him for ages and he totally evades my questions every time."

"What is it with men?"

"I have no idea. This calls for one thing."

"And that would be?"

"Cocktails. There's a wine bar a few blocks down. But—"

"Not to worry. I can't deal with Tomas now. I'll tell him I need to spend some quality time with my best friend."

"And I need some liquid courage before Davison gets home, especially if there's going to be a repeat of that performance."

"Men…" we mutter simultaneously, shaking our heads simultaneously in frustration.

Chapter Fifteen

DAVISON

*P*lausible deniability.

That's the way I rationalize how I'm dealing with Allegra in terms of my father's situation and the threats. It's my form of protection. I know I pissed her off when I called yesterday desperate to know where she was. But I needed to know she was safe. I managed to calm myself down and not come home agitated.

And now I'm making it up to her, her gorgeous body nestled into mine on the couch, watching a movie of her choosing, *A Room with a View*, to make up for the phone call.

I wasn't too interested in it because I was more focused on Allegra—stroking her hair, caressing her soft flesh under my Harvard sweatshirt.

"Pay attention! This is the best part. George kisses Lucy in the poppy field!" she tells me, all excited.

She grips my hand as I glance at the screen. I have to admit that it actually is a beautiful camera shot of the actors in a field with red poppies sprinkled throughout the tall grass.

"I love that scene," she says dreamily, sounding like a true fan. "It's so romantic."

"I guess," I murmur.

"How come you don't do romantic shit like that for me?"

My head rears back in surprise. "Excuse me?"

With my finger under her chin, I tilt her head toward me. A mischievous grin is spread across her face, with her eyes directed away from me, waiting for my reaction.

I start tickling her. "Say you're sorry," I order her as she squirms and fidgets like a fish out of water, screaming as she begs me to stop.

"Okay, okay, I'm sorry!" she shouts. She falls back on my lap, her legs on top of my thighs with her breath panting.

Her deep brown eyes stare back at me, alive and full of laughter. "I should punish you some more," I tell her.

She smirks at me knowingly. "But perhaps something more, shall we say, of a sensual nature?"

"I love the way you think, Venus."

Just as I'm reaching under her sweatpants for her sweet pussy, my cell rings.

We both groan at the same time.

I reach over for my phone on the coffee table and see Ian Parker's name on my screen. "What is it, Ian?" I ask, slightly annoyed.

"Sir, I'm really sorry to bother you, but I wanted to tell you right away."

"And that would be?"

I can hear him take a deep breath before he speaks again. "I started my own research, analyzing the quarterly reports of the last twelve months."

Exactly what I had been doing, but I hadn't finished yet. Interesting.

"And none of my numbers match what went into the final copies."

My heart starts to beat faster as my pulse races with worry.

"Are you sure? Didn't you work on the numbers since you've worked for me?"

"No, sir. This is the first one that Mr. Craig assigned me to. And I found something else. Something that came to me today in an interoffice envelope. I don't know where it came from because my name was the only one on it."

"What?" I demand insistently.

"You need to see it for yourself, because I'm not exactly sure what it is."

I don't like the sound of this.

"Send me everything right now, but not to my Berkeley Holdings account," I tell him hurriedly. "I'll give you my personal e-mail."

I recite my e-mail address to him.

"Okay, done," he confirms.

"Good. I'll go check right now. Keep me posted. And do not tell anyone you've done this."

"I won't," he promises. "Good night, sir."

"Good night, Parker. And thank you."

We hang up. Allegra is looking at me, slightly scared. "What's wrong, Davison?"

"Nothing. I need to check something on my computer."

I start to lift her off my lap, but she sits up, allowing me to rise from the couch. Once I get to my office, I power on my laptop and scroll through my e-mail.

Ian sent me an Excel file comparing his numbers with the official data from the reports we filed. They're off. By a huge margin.

Then I open the other document he sent me. It's a scan of a prospectus letter on Berkeley Holdings letterhead, dated about eighteen months ago.

The top of the letter has AN EXCLUSIVE INVESTMENT OPPORTUNITY! GUARANTEED MILLIONS TO BE MADE!

I quickly scan the letter. Phrases like "bio oil drilling in Louisiana," "new wells discovered," and "huge profits to be made" pop out at me.

When I reach the bottom, only one name is used as the signatory.

DOMINIC CRAIG, CHIEF FINANCIAL OFFICER, BERKELEY HOLDINGS

That motherfucker.

I print everything out and turn off the laptop. I grab my sneakers and wallet from the bedroom, heading back to the living room.

Allegra instantly sits up from where she is lying on the couch and starts asking me questions. "Davison, what's going on? Who was that? And what are you holding in your hand?"

Not now, baby. Please.

"I gotta go."

Her mouth drops as she shoots to her feet. "Are you kidding me? Christ, Davison, what the fuck is going on with you?"

I step closer to her and kiss her on the forehead. I lean back to look into her eyes. *I can't have this touch you. Touch us. Please, for your sake, let it go, Allegra.*

I turn and head for the door, not daring to turn around because I can't bear to see the hurt in Allegra's eyes.

* * *

As Charles speeds up the FDR to my parents' house, I call to make sure he's at home.

Ames, our family butler, answers in his crisp patrician voice. "Berkeley residence."

"Ames, is my father at home?" I demand from him.

"Yes, sir."

"Good. I'll be right there. Don't tell him."

"Of course. I'll be waiting for your arrival."

"Thanks, Ames."

Charles stops the Maybach in front of my family home in Sutton Square. I rush up to the door, with Ames already opening it for me.

"Where is he?"

"His study," Ames quickly replies.

I race down the hall and burst through the door. My father is sitting in his leather desk chair with his back to me, looking out the window at our backyard garden. I don't even think he hears me come in. He's not yelling or telling me that I should learn how to knock. A crystal tumbler of Scotch is sitting on his desk. Something is off.

"Dad?"

"Hello, Davison," he replies, his voice sounding somewhat dispirited.

"I need to show you something."

He spins his chair around, and I finally see him. He's not wearing a suit as I expected him to, but a T-shirt and dress pants under a button-down cardigan sweater. His face is drawn and his eyes are sunken.

I step forward and place the papers in front of him on his desk. He reaches for them, giving them a brief glance. He doesn't look up at me. I decide to tread carefully with him because I don't think shouting will get what I need from him, which are answers.

"Dad, you need to tell me what's going on."

"Sit down," he tells me in a steady voice, and like the dutiful son, I do as I'm told.

My father reaches for his drink, takes a long sip, and then begins to speak.

"Some time ago, Ashton's father, Malcolm, asked me to go in with him on an investment opportunity. He found out about it from these three businessmen in Chicago who asked if he wanted to go partners with them. They offered him a chance to make a lot of money drilling for bio oil in the South."

My stomach begins to churn with unease as my skin starts to crawl. I know what's coming. I'm not going to say it for him. I want the foul words to come out of his own mouth.

"But it was all a scam. There was no bio oil drilling. When you walked in on me at the office, Malcolm had just told me that the Chicago partners had ties to the Mob. He swore to me the ties were loose, but he hadn't done any due diligence. They were still connected to them. And to make it worse, the investment targeted senior citizens. They'd give us their life savings and not get anything in return."

"That explains the prospectus letter," I reconcile.

"What letter?"

"Look at the document on the bottom."

He pulls out the doc. As he reads it, his face turns red, his jaw clenching tightly.

"I can't believe it! Dominic, that fucking bastard!" he shouts.

"Yeah, and from what I can tell, he's been embezzling from the company."

"What are you talking about?" he asks, genuinely shocked.

"Ian Parker found discrepancies in the quarterly reports, which he brought to my attention. From what I can tell, he's been doing it for months. Are you telling me you didn't know anything about this?"

"Of course not! Do you think I would've approved of this?" he counters.

I grit my teeth and my blood is boiling with fury when I jump to my feet.

"Yeah, at this point I do, because you've lost your goddamned mind, Dad!" I scream at him. "Do you know how many laws you've broken? Jesus Christ, I can't believe you! Are you that greedy, that desperate for money and power? Did you honestly think you were going to get away with this? Do you understand the shit storm that will fall on *me* because of what you've done? I could go to prison. Not to mention that they're threatening Allegra."

My father jumps to his feet in fury. "Last time I checked, you're the one who should've been on top of this, but instead, you were busy screwing that Italian gold digger!"

My rage erupts as I grab his glass and smash it against the wall. "Say that to me again! I fucking dare you!"

He retreats from me, worry reflecting back at me in his eyes.

Judging by his reaction, my message came through loud and clear. "Good, we understand each other. I just have one thing to say to you. Either go to the Feds and tell them everything or I will. Three days, Dad. Three days and then I'm going myself, with or without you."

I walk out of my father's office and the house without a word to anyone. I signal to Charles to stay put in the Maybach, and he acknowledges me with a nod. I can't go home yet. Instead, I turn left on Sutton Place South, hitting East Fifty-Seventh Street and heading for Sutton Place Park, which overlooks the East River. I plop down onto a bench and look out across the water to Queens. I try to comprehend everything that just happened, everything that my father just told me. My head can't stop spinning. The repercussions of his actions and how they'll affect Berkeley Holdings make me sick to my stomach.

Suddenly, I need to hear her voice. I need to know that someone as good and caring as Allegra loves me for who I am and not my financial worth.

When I pull out my cell, I see a missed text from her: *If you really do love me, you have a funny way of showing it. I'm going home. Have a good night.*

My head falls back onto the bench.

Goddamn it, Allegra. Why can't you just trust me?

* * *

ALLEGRA

I guess I shouldn't be surprised when I see Davison's Maybach waiting for me across from Le Bistro when I finish my shift the following night. I ignored his texts all day because I am so frustrated with him and I didn't want to bring a bad attitude to work. Why is he hiding things from me? That's not what partners do. And that's what we are…or what I thought we were.

I managed to stay professional all night, but I wasn't feeling particularly social with the staff. I just kept to myself, keeping my eyes on the clock, desperate for my shift to end so I could go home. I knew it would be pointless to argue against him giving me a lift home, so I just slide into my seat when Charles opens the door for me.

Davison is sitting in his usual spot. The car carries his familiar scent—his spicy aftershave with male sweat, despite the cooled air inside. He finally speaks to me when we near Forty-Second Street.

"Why didn't you answer any of my texts?" he demands.

When I look over at him, his eyes are searing into mine. He is so exasperating. "For someone with two Harvard degrees, you can be so obtuse. Because I'm pissed at you."

"Do you honestly think I would've ditched you if it wasn't important?"

"Then tell me where you went," I snap back at him. *Please just tell me the truth.*

"I had to see my father."

Okay. Wasn't expecting that. "Why?"

He sighs. "I can't tell you."

I throw up my hands. "Of course you can't." I press the intercom in the panel next to me. "Charles, take me home, please."

"What the hell are you doing?" he shouts. He turns to the intercom on his side of the car. "Home, Charles. My home. *Our* home."

I know that last reference was directed to me.

I hear Charles's voice over the speaker. "Yes, sir."

I can't handle this anymore. I turn to him so I can look straight into his eyes. "Davison, do you remember what Dr. Turner told us about how we need to be honest and communicate with each other for our relationship to survive? So tell me right now what's going on or you can pull the car over and I'll get home on my own."

His jaw clenches as his eyes grow fiery with anger. "Damn it, Allegra. It's for your own good."

"How is keeping secrets good for me? Good for *us*? You have to trust me."

"I'm just protecting you!" he yells back at me.

I shake my head. "How is lying to me protecting me?"

I take a deep breath. I don't even know if he heard me.

"Take me home, Davison. Please," I manage, barely above a whisper.

A pause, then I hear his voice. "Charles, we're taking Miss Orsini home."

"Very well, sir," the older man replies.

I can't even look at him, staring out the window as the city flies past the car. When we reach Mulberry Street, I allow him to help me out of the door as he always does. He walks behind me until I reach the door of my building. I look into my purse, rummaging for my keys.

Without warning, his right index finger lifts my chin so he can look at me in the eyes. He softly kisses my lips, then pulls back. "I love you, Allegra. Don't ever forget that."

I still for a moment before his voice stirs me. "Did you find your keys?"

I lift my hand out of my purse, not even realizing I've been holding on to them the entire time. I present them to him in silent reply.

"Good. I'll wait until you're inside," he says, not touching me again.

I look up into his emerald eyes, heavy with concern and worry. I peck him quickly on the lips so he knows that I heard every word he said.

Turning my back on him, I open the door, shutting it firmly behind me.

When I walk into my apartment, Papa is in the living room, reading a book. "*Cara*, what are you doing home? I thought you'd be staying over at Davison's house."

I sink down on the couch next to him. "We had a fight. He's keeping something from me and he won't tell me what it is."

My father lets out a small sigh. "You're being ridiculous. Did you ever think he has a good reason for doing that?"

"Maybe he does, but I wish he trusted me enough to tell me."

"Then give him the benefit of the doubt. He loves you, Allegra. Don't punish him for wanting to protect you," he admonishes me.

I glance over at my father—my very wise father. I hug him tightly and plant a kiss on his cheek. "I'll try, Papa. *Grazie.*"

"*Bene.* Now go get some sleep."

I peck him on the cheek again. "I will. *Buona notte.*"

"Good night, *cara.*"

I lift myself off the sofa and head for my bedroom. I collapse onto my bed and mentally review the past twenty-four hours.

And then I know what I have to do.

Chapter Sixteen

It killed me dropping off Allegra at her place last night. I didn't want to upset her further, so I did as she asked me. I don't want to keep going on like this with her, but I have no choice if I'm going to protect her from the shit storm that my father created. After everything she went through when that scum Morandi kidnapped her, the last thing she needs to know right now is that she's under threat again because of something that's happening with my family and me. Dr. Turner is helping her get past everything with their therapy sessions, and I refuse to make it worse for her. I'm not going to tell her anything because it's the only way to keep her safe.

Which explains why I look like total hell when I wake up this morning. I barely slept at all, and my energy level is completely depleted. I rub my eyes with the heels of my hands as I pad into my kitchen. I don't even bother to put on boxers or sweats.

I left my cell on the counter last night. When I check it, there are no calls or texts from Allegra.

Fuck.

I slam the phone down on the granite, not giving two shits if I break the damn thing. I start fumbling around in my cabinets for the coffee filters, shoving one inside the pot. I reach for the coffee from the fridge, but when I open the bag, I pull it so hard that the grinds go flying everywhere like fucking confetti.

I hurl the bag into the air, roaring in absolute frustration. I lean against the fridge, letting the metal cool my raging body. My head falls back as I attempt to take a deep breath.

When my heartbeat finally begins to regulate, I hear the familiar *ding* from my elevator. I take a few steps into the foyer.

Allegra is standing in front of me, dressed in her favorite Gotham Conservatory sweatshirt, the jean shorts she wore all the time when we were in Lake Como, and black flip-flops on her feet, her beautiful tanned legs shown off to perfection and her soft brown hair falling around her face.

Those luminous eyes of hers that I could stare at forever are looking right at me, as if they could see into my fucking soul.

She only says two words to me. "Make-up sex."

Before I can move, she rushes to me within seconds and jumps straight into my arms. With her legs locked around me, I grab her head and slam her lips to mine.

She tastes so sweet, so delicious. This is my life. *She* is my life. She is what I savor. She is the sustenance I need to keep going.

Without releasing her mouth, I rush for the bedroom with her luscious body coiled around me. She is warm in my arms, her delicious coconut scent filling my nose. I can sense her flip-flops falling off her feet behind me as I race down the hallway.

I plant her down on the floor and start yanking off her clothes, with her unzipping her shorts as I pull her sweatshirt over her head.

She scrambles onto the bed, positioning herself on her back, her eyes blazing with desire and her legs spread-eagled, as ready, eager, and hungry for me as I am for her. She doesn't say a word, but she doesn't have to, because we both want and need the same thing.

This is going to be raw, primal, and rough, and I can't wait to be inside her.

She reaches out to me, silently pleading for my body on top of hers. When I collapse on top of her, her hands wrap around my head, and she plunges her tongue into my mouth. We tangle like that until I feel sated from the taste of her, but I need so much more.

I slide down to take her breasts into my mouth, pushing them together so I can lick them simultaneously. I bite down on the succulent flesh as her moans grow louder. "Oh God…Davison…don't stop…just don't stop…please," she begs. I can hear the desperation in her voice, dying for that release only I can give her.

I grunt in reply, frenzied with lust, wanting to taste every inch of her.

My tongue leaves a trail of worship behind as I move down her body, licking around the circle of her navel. Finally, I reach her pussy, glistening in the morning sunlight.

I dive into her with my tongue, first swirling it around to lick her clean, then full-on with my mouth, devouring her like a beast feeding on its kill, except Allegra is alive and breathing, and all mine.

Her voice spurs me on, her rapturous appeals not to stop, telling me how good my mouth feels on her cunt. Her body begins to shudder from the orgasm overtaking her. I hold her legs in place as they shake and spasm with aftershocks.

I rise from my feast and slip off the bed, standing at the edge. Without warning her, I pull Allegra's feet to me, listening to her gasp in surprise. I place her ankles on my shoulders, arranging her perfectly as I sink my cock into her, wet and ready for me. She inhales deeply from the sensation, my shaft swelling from the mere sound of it.

I start thrusting inside her, holding her steady with my hands gripping her legs. I grunt with each rough drive into her, her pussy tight on my cock like a steel vise.

"Let me hear you, baby," I command her.

Her deep moans make me piston her faster. "Do you like that? Do you like it raw and hard?"

"Oh God, yes, Davison…"

"Do you want me to go faster?"

"Fuck yes! Please!" she begs.

With those three words, I fuck her harder, the bed shaking violently from my continuous thrusts.

We're both so close. My eyes are shut in anticipation. I cannot wait to hear her cry my name in ecstasy.

"Now, Allegra," I order her, my voice rough and demanding.

She screams, shattering me as I hear her yell my name in worship. My cock still inside her, her cunt milks it until my orgasm follows hers, my legs trembling and my breath panting for fresh oxygen.

When I glance down at her, I watch as her chest rises and falls, then she crooks her finger at me, inviting me to come to her.

I collapse down next to her, both of us on our backs, our bodies mirroring each other in panting breaths. I lay my hand on hers, to maintain the connection of what we just did to each other, *for* each other. She grips it instantly.

She turns on her side to face me. "I'm sorry," she says to me as her breathing slowly returns to normal.

I roll over to look into her softened eyes. "Whatever for, baby?"

"For not understanding. I know you can't tell me what's going on, as much as I wish you would. You probably have a good reason to keep it from me."

"You're right. I do."

"But I also know that I need to trust you."

I stroke her cheek with the pads of my fingers. "You can trust me. You know that. What caused this sudden realization?"

"Let's just say a very wise man reminded me of some things and gave me a wake-up call."

"Your father?"

She smiles. "Yup."

"A wise man indeed," I reply, grinning back at her. "I'm only trying to protect you."

She leans in and kisses me softly on the lips. "I accept that. I still wish you could tell me why I need protection."

"So do I, my love. So do I," I answer, returning her kiss.

Chapter Seventeen

DAVISON

The next morning, I'm in the kitchen prepping my coffee while Allegra is getting dressed. My cell rings from the counter. Ashton's name appears on the caller ID.

"Ashton, what's wrong? Did you get any more phone calls?" I ask worriedly when I pick up.

"No," she replies calmly. "My father finally told me everything. I can't believe he did this. And then he got your father involved…" She sighs. "I just wanted to check in with you. Anything new on your end?"

I decide not to tell her about Dominic since that involves my company, not her.

"Nothing to report. My father's being a stubborn ass. I told him he has to turn himself in to the Feds, but he refuses. This is such a clusterfuck."

"I know. I'll do the best I can with my father as well."

"All right, Ashton. Keep me posted."

"Will do. Thank you, Davison."

I hang up and tuck my phone into my suit trousers. I exhale, falling back against the cold metal of my fridge.

"Davison?"

I turn to her, her purse hanging from her shoulder, ready to leave. Her eyes are fixed on me with concern.

"Is everything okay?" she whispers.

I step toward her and take her in my arms. I caress her jaw with my right hand as we're wrapped in each other.

"Yes, baby. Everything is fine. Are we good?" I ask her nervously.

A slight smile takes over her face. "Yes, Harvard, we're good. It's not that I don't trust you, because you know I do."

"I know, but it's good to hear that now and again."

She strokes the back of my neck. "I just don't want you to get hurt by whatever it is that's going on with you."

I wish I could tell her it's not me that I'm frightened for, but her.

"I'll be fine, I promise," I reassure her.

She nods. "Okay, I'd better go. I've got the dinner shift tonight."

"I'll see you after," I remind her.

She leans in to kiss me good-bye, a long, wet kiss that threatens to take us over with its heat, but she pulls back before our desire for each other escalates because we both know we have busy days ahead of us—she has her shift, and I have to get to the office and figure out what to do about my father.

"I love you, baby," I whisper, leaning my forehead on hers.

"I love you too. And I used the last of your half-and-half with my coffee, so you need to get some more," she informs me.

"Yes, dear," I reply, sounding like the devoted boyfriend I am.

She smiles back at me. "See you later," she says to me before pressing the elevator button, and disappearing behind the metal doors.

I head back into the kitchen and start to put our breakfast dishes in the dishwasher when I hear the elevator open again.

I hustle back into the foyer, excited to see her again, ready to scoop her up into my arms. "Back for round two, Venus?"

But instead of Allegra, my mother is standing in front of the elevator, shaking her head. "I'm not even going to ask what any of that means."

I wince in pain when she says that.

Crap.

"Oh…Mom…hi…it's just that Allegra…" I stammer like a teenage boy busted by his mother for jerking off in his room, despite the fact that I'm a grown man.

She waves her hand at me dismissively. "Don't bother, darling. I ran into Allegra downstairs." She steps up to me to give me a hug and kiss on the cheek.

Her appearance has me unsettled to say the least. "What's going on?"

"Let's sit down," she says to me in a calm voice.

I follow her into my living room. She sits down on my couch, and I join her, taking in her appearance. She's dressed in a black cashmere sweater set with white linen pants and black open-toed sandals, her elegant wardrobe contrasting against the rest of her when I notice her hands fidgeting and she's crossing her legs over and over.

I clamp my hands over hers to keep them still. "Mom, what's going on? I've never seen you like this before."

After a pause, she shifts her head to look directly at me. "I want you to tell me what's going on with your father."

Shit.

"What do you mean?" I ask cautiously to assess what she knows.

"Davison, my darling son, pardon my French, but don't bullshit me. I know something is wrong because Ames overheard you and your father arguing."

My mother may be a lady of genteel society, but when Mona Cabot Berkeley uses an expletive, she's not fucking around.

I'm stunned. "I can't believe Ames, being that indiscreet."

"He likes me better than your father," she states as if it were a fact that I should already be aware of for some reason. "Now tell me everything."

I inhale deeply and nod my head. "Okay."

And then I tell her the whole sordid story—Ashton's father involving my father in his scheme, their Chicago partners having ties to the Mob, bilking the pensioners. All of it.

When I finish, my mother's hands clench into fists. She shoots up from the sofa and starts pacing the floor. "I can't believe him!" she shouts. "How disgusting! How could he do that to those poor people! What a bastard!"

Suddenly, she stops moving to look over at me. The fire of anger that was blazing from them a second ago is now extinguished, and I only see one thing in them—fear.

"What are we going to do, Davison?"

My heart breaks for my mother, this woman who has been nothing but a model of civility and kindness in my life, as opposed to my father, a man whose prime motivations in life are greed and power.

I jump to my feet to comfort her. "I'm taking care of it," I tell her soothingly. "I told Dad that if he wasn't going to the Feds to confess, I would do it instead. You didn't know any of this was going on, so you're not to blame in any way. And don't worry, because I'll take care of you no matter what happens. I swear it."

She grabs me in a tight embrace. "I know you will, because you're a good son. You're the one thing I've done right in my life."

When I pull back, I see her eyes moistened and on the verge of tears. I grab a tissue from the box on the coffee table, handing it to her. "Please don't cry, Mom. Everything will be all right."

She wipes her eyes daintily so as not to ruin her makeup. "Thank you, darling. I think I'll go home. It's such a lovely day outside. Maybe I'll pick a few roses from the garden, do some flower arranging. That'll calm me down."

I smile at her. "Sounds like a good idea."

She steps over to retrieve her purse from the couch and takes my hand as she walks to the elevator. Before she leaves, she pecks me on the cheek and gives me one final hug.

"Just promise me you'll keep me informed and keep yourself safe."

I grip her shoulders firmly. "I promise."

She blows me a kiss from the elevator as the doors close on her. I start to walk toward the bedroom when I remember what Allegra told me. I pull on a pair of shoes, grabbing my wallet, keys, and phone to head down to the market around the corner.

I steer around the building into the narrow alley when a rough male voice stops me. "Allegra looked so cute in those shorts this morning. And she looked hot at Le Bistro. Wish I could get a piece of that."

I freeze in place. It's the bastard who approached Allegra at work. When I finally do turn around, I come face to face with a guy in a suit who looks like a normal guy, save for the menacing look in his blue eyes, his lips firmly pursed together. My blood starts to run cold as my heart starts pounding so hard that I can feel my pulse beating in the arteries against my neck.

I grab him by the throat, using my hold on him to hurl him into the wall of my apartment building. My hand is still wrapped around him, now with my other hand pressing his shoulder into the concrete.

"You fucking asshole! If you so much—"

"I would remove my hands if I were you, Mr. Berkeley."

He flips open his suit jacket to reveal a holster with a handgun strapped inside it.

I quickly release him, watching him straighten his jacket and wiping off his shoulder as if my touch had tainted the fabric. "Your father's partners in Chicago have no scruples in removing any impediment to getting what they want, or doing what they need to send him a warning to comply with their wishes."

I'm paralyzed, watching this asshole's mouth move, desperate to pummel him to the ground, but with him armed, I can't take that chance.

He smiles at me like a madman. "Have a nice day," he rasps to me.

I pivot slightly to see him walk away and turn the corner.

I rip my phone from the pocket of my sweats and scroll furiously for a number. "Charles!"

"I'm in front. Ready when you are, sir."

"It's not that. I'll cab it to work today. I need you to do something much more important."

* * *

ALLEGRA

It's moments like these when I'm grateful for my love of opera. A day later, I'm practicing with Luciana at Davison's apartment, which manages to keep my mind off Davison and that phone call he got from Ashton. I heard him say her name at the end, and I was ready to go ballistic, demanding to know why he was talking to her. But I calmed down, reminding myself that I had to trust him. I couldn't let the call distract me. With the district tryouts approaching soon for the Metropolitan Opera National Council Auditions, I need to be ready.

Once Lucy and I finish, we head over to Tribeca for lunch at a diner on Greenwich Street that Davison and I like to go to on the weekends. And for once, I'm happy to hear about someone else's problems with their love life rather than complaining about my own.

"I don't get it, Alli," Lucy laments over her tuna melt. "Tomas has been so moody lately. Whenever I press him about it, he either gets all sullen or rages at me like a lion with a damn thorn in its paw."

"Do you have any guesses about what it might be?"

"Well, he's not cheating, that's for damn sure, because he knows I wouldn't cry about it. Instead, I'd remove his entire package with a fucking blowtorch."

I try to suppress my laughter at her blunt comment, knowing she's not joking around. She really would do that. "I agree with you there. He worships the ground you walk on."

"And believe me, it would be a shame to do that, because the man is a beast in bed. He does this thing—"

I drop the fork I'm holding to eat my chicken Caesar salad and hold up my hand to her. "It's okay. I believe you. Sounds like the denial thing is going around because Davison is keeping something from me as well, but I won't press him about it. Not anymore, anyway. I trust him."

She takes a sip of her Diet Coke. "Don't they get that we're only trying to help? That we nag them because we love them?"

"'Love'? Are you there already?" I ask her, my eyebrows raised.

A huge grin of a besotted woman overtakes Lucy's face. "Yeah. Ever since the night of the benefit at Davison's parents' house. He was so sweet with me that night, and when he saved the day taking that video of Davison going apeshit on that skank Ashton, he became my hero."

I shake my head in disbelief. "Never thought I'd see the day."

"I know. It's a fucking miracle," she laughs. "And that sexy accent doesn't hurt either. I lose it when we're in bed and he says—"

"Got it," I reply with a mouthful of salad.

"Ugh. Really, Alli? Did you not learn the last time you did that in front of me? You know what I'm going to say."

I roll my eyes. "Manners."

* * *

I decide to kill some time after lunch at Barnes and Noble on the next block before I head home. As I'm reading a magazine in the store's café, a male voice says, "Excuse me, is this seat taken?" When I look up, Matteo is smiling and standing in front of me.

I smile back in surprise. "Hey! What are you doing here?"

He sits down across from me. "I've got a job interview with a graphic designer at her loft a few blocks from here. Hopefully, she'll like me enough to make me her assistant."

"I'm sure she will," I reassure him.

"What brings you here?" he asks.

I take a sip of my latte. "Davison's apartment is nearby. I was there this morning, then had lunch with a friend."

He nods his head. "So, how are things going with him?" I can tell he's nervous asking me that question.

"We're good. Things have been weird with him and it drove me crazy for a while, but I realize I just have to trust him."

His head falls as he finds something fascinating in his coffee.

"What is it, Matteo?"

"As much as it kills me to say it, I could tell how much he loves you when I met him in Italy. He had no qualms marking his territory when it came to you."

I grit my teeth, being referred to as "territory." "Davison can be intense sometimes."

He sighs. "Look, it's a guy thing. He's your boyfriend and you love him, and I respect that. But just know that I'll always be here for you."

"Thanks. I appreciate that."

He glances at his watch. "Crap. I'd better go. I'm glad I ran into you."

"Me too. Good luck today. And take care."

He stands up and steps to me, leaning over to peck me on the cheek. "See ya," he says, walking away with his coffee.

I take a deep breath and finish my latte. When I stand up to throw the cup into the garbage, a flash of a man with white hair under a black cap catches my eye. He has his back to me as he's standing in the history section, but I know who it is without having to see him from the front. He turns slightly and looks over in my direction, and just as quickly twists back around.

What the hell?

With my purse slung over my shoulder, I march over to him, my curiosity increasing with each step.

"You can turn around, Charles. I saw you."

I can hear him exhale deeply before he spins around to face me, his pale face red with embarrassment. "Hello, Miss Orsini."

"What's going on, Charles? I'm assuming you're not here by accident."

He shuts his eyes before answering me. "That would be correct, ma'am."

"Then why are you here?"

This time, he looks me straight in the eye. "Because Mr. Berkeley told me to watch over you."

I clench my teeth. "Why?"

"I don't know, and that's the truth."

"That, I believe all too well."

Now that I know *she* is most likely involved in all this somehow, my patience with Davison is wearing thin, close to dissipating altogether. I rush out of the store, not even needing to look back to know that Charles is behind me, matching me step for step.

Once I get outside, I snatch my cell from my purse. He picks up on the first ring.

"Hey," Davison says to me sweetly.

"Why is Charles following me? And how long has he been doing it?" I demand from him, not even bothering with any pleasantries.

"I can't tell you. And to answer your second question, since yesterday."

"Tell me the fuck why, Davison!"

I hear him groan. "For chrissakes, Allegra, just for once can you just back off and stop asking so many questions? I'm handling it!"

"There it is again! 'It,' 'it,' 'it'! If you really do trust me, then why can't you tell me what 'it' is?"

"Because I can't," he replies in that tone that doesn't welcome debate.

Tears of anger and frustration begin to fill my eyes. "I gotta go," I manage as my voice cracks.

"Allegra, wait—"

I hang up before he can finish his sentence.

I lean back against the building to catch my breath and collect myself. I need answers. I can't ask his parents. Charles doesn't know anything.

And then I think of the one person I can ask, as much as it'll kill me to do it. A root canal without painkillers would be less torturous.

Suck it up. This is for Davison.

I start walking east determinedly with Charles close behind, ignoring my phone that is persistently vibrating in my purse because I know it's Davison trying to reach me. If I hear his voice now, I know what will happen. I'll break down in tears and completely lose my nerve.

"Umm, Miss Orsini, where are you going?" he asks, a bit out of breath to catch up with me.

"Someplace that I really don't want to go, but I have no choice."

"Then let me get the Maybach and I'll drive you."

"I'm taking the subway, Charles. Either come with me or I'm leaving you behind."

He takes one long, deep breath. "Then I guess I have no other choice, do I?" he concludes.

* * *

As the uptown 6 barrels along Lexington Avenue, I glance up at Charles from my spot on the long plastic bench inside the train. I never realized how tall he was until now, hovering over me, his eyes constantly moving and watching the other passengers. Protecting me.

He has always been kind to me ever since I started seeing Davison, and I want to know more about him, since he is such an important part of Davison's life.

"Charles, may I ask you a question?"

"Certainly, Miss Orsini."

"Are you married?"

He smiles slightly at my inquiry, his eyes shutting briefly. "Millicent. My Millie."

I tilt my head at him curiously. "How long have you been together?"

"We were married for thirty years, but we were friends before that. We grew up across the street from each other in Brooklyn."

His use of the word "were" does not escape my attention. "Has she passed away?"

"Two years ago. Cancer. It was horrible. Mr. Berkeley was very kind and supportive, making sure Millie had the best doctors and hospice care. He let me take as much time as I needed with her. I was lucky to be with her when she took her last breath."

A small tear escapes my eye. "Did you have children?"

He shakes his head. "We tried for a long time, but we decided that it wasn't in our plan, so we just loved each other to the fullest. But I have lots of nieces and nephews, so we always enjoyed their company at the holidays."

"I wish I could've known her."

"She would've liked you very much, Miss Orsini. You remind me a lot of her."

My heart softens at his comment. "How so?"

"You are just as strong and obstinate as she was, but more than that, you are fiercely loyal and protective of those you love."

"Davison…"

He nods. "You've changed him. He used to be so cold and humorless, but I knew deep down he was just waiting for the right woman to show up. The one who would make him happy."

"I hope you mean me," I reply nervously.

He laughs and smiles at me. "Yes, Miss Orsini. I mean you."

"Just checking." I laugh in return.

* * *

Stepping out on Lexington and Seventy-Seventh Street, we head west for Madison Avenue. "At this time of day, she'll probably be either at Sant Ambroeus or Swifty's," Charles surmises, naming two of the popular restaurants Ashton and her society circle frequent the most for lunch. "Let's try Sant Ambroeus first since it's closest. Then we can head down for the other if she's not there."

"Thank you for doing this, Charles."

"Davison is like a son to me, Miss Orsini," he announces, a statement that says everything I need to know about how he feels about his employer.

We reach the café, and I instantly spot her inside. She looks over to the window and freezes when she sees my face.

A warm hand grips my arm. "Let me go in first," Charles offers. "I'll ask her to come outside. We don't want to make a scene."

"If anyone was going to make a scene, it would be her, not me. I'll wait here."

I watch apprehensively as Charles walks in, making his way to Ashton and her friends. His tall frame bends over as he whispers in her ear. As he speaks to her, I can see her eyes focused on mine, blazing in anger.

Then she plasters a fake smile onto her face, delicately wipes the corners of her mouth, and rises from her chair. I move away from the window so as not to give her friends and the rest of the café patrons a show.

I take a deep breath as Ashton walks over to me, my fists clenching and releasing. Dressed in a pale pink linen sundress with matching sandals and a Lilly Pulitzer scarf wrapped around her neck, she is the epitome of a WASP princess.

She stops about a foot away from me. "Hello, Allegra. I have to say it's a surprise to see you here, but even more with Charles. Davison not good enough for you?"

I roll my eyes. *That old adage about a leopard never changing its spots? Too fucking right.*

Charles plants himself just a few steps away with his back to us, again watching and scanning. Protecting me.

"Now," Ashton says to me, her voice not disguising her contempt for me, "what could possibly be so important to interrupt my time with my friends?"

Okay, Orsini. Showtime.

"You need to stay away from Davison. He's going through enough without you."

She pauses before speaking again and sighs. "Believe me, there's nothing I'd like more than to be out of his life completely, because that would mean I wouldn't be in yours either. But, like it or not, our fathers are in this together, which means I'm involved. I'm just trying to help him. What has he told you so far?"

Okay, she knows everything, so just play along.

"Only his side of it. Now I need to hear yours."

She moves closer to the building, indicating she doesn't want the entire Upper East Side to hear what she's about to tell me. "Very well."

I follow her lead, standing inches apart now, as she begins to speak. "My father got Davison's father involved in the scheme with these businessmen from Chicago to drill for bio oil, bilking pensioners for their life savings by telling them they'd make a ton of money. The Chicago men used Berkeley Holdings as a legit front thanks to Dominic, their CFO. Then my father found out the guys had ties to the Mob. So now, Davison and I are trying to convince both of them to go to the Feds and tell them everything."

I'm keeping a straight face, nodding along to pretend I know all this already, but inside, I'm screaming and cringing with each word coming out of Ashton's mouth.

"Then my father started getting strange phone calls threatening him, which I happened to hear once when I picked up the line by mistake. I went to Davison and told him, and now I don't know what's happening. The phone calls have stopped, as far as I know."

"When did the phone calls start with your father?"

"I guess about a month and a half or so ago."

Right around the time when I was in Italy.

"Does that sound similar to what Davison told you?" she asks, watching me for my reaction.

"Pretty much," I lie through my teeth.

"If that's all, I'm going to join my friends," she announces, her back already facing me.

"Of course. Thank you for speaking with me. I appreciate it."

I'm about to tell Charles that I'm ready to go, when Ashton calls my name. "Allegra, you didn't know anything until I told you just now, did you?"

What the hell. It's not like I'm planning to see her again.

I turn around to face her one last time. "No, I didn't," I confess.

She crosses her arms. "Wow. You're smarter than I thought you were. It must've killed you to come here to talk to me."

I swallow in my throat. "You'd be correct with that assumption. However, there's nothing I wouldn't do to protect him."

I finally reach Charles, but not before Ashton addresses me one last time.

"You must really love Davison."

I look back at her, directly in the eyes so she'll get the full effect of what I'm about to tell her with no chance of misinterpretation.

"I'd take a bullet for him."

Chapter Eighteen

The only other time I can recall being this nervous to see Allegra was when I went to see her at her father's butcher shop to ask for her forgiveness when she saw me with Ashton at the Met and thought I was cheating on her behind her back. But this is worse because as happy as I will be to see her, I have information which Charles passed on to me that I'm not thrilled about in the slightest. She texted me a few hours ago that she needed to see me ASAP.

Too fucking right.

The elevator's bell signals her arrival. Today was a scorcher of a summer day in New York City, the kind that makes all five boroughs one giant sauna. She steps out in a tight white cotton dress, the one she was wearing when I saw her singing in La Diva's garden, and her flip-flops, her hair pulled back in a ponytail.

At the sight of each other, the same words in a matching

tone of frustration spill simultaneously from our mouths: "Why didn't you tell me?"

We both laugh nervously, though I think I have more reason to be angry at this moment, regardless of what she has to tell me.

"Do you want to go first?" I ask.

"I suppose. Let's get this over with."

Taking her hand, I lead us over to the living room, settling us down on the sofa. She doesn't let go of me, staring right at me, her soft brown eyes steady. "You should've told me about your father's scheme with Ashton's father. It would've kept me from thinking stupid shit, like a fleeting thought I had that you were losing interest in me."

Oh, baby, what the fuck?

I rear back in shock, my heart dropping at her confession. "Are you kidding me? You can't honestly think that would ever happen."

"I said it was a fleeting thought, Harvard, so relax."

"Fine. But she told you everything?"

She sighs. "Yes. Except now I need to know why you had Charles following me around for the last twenty-four hours."

I'm frightened to tell her, but I can't keep anything from her. Not anymore.

"I received several anonymous phone calls, and in the last one, the man said some untoward things in reference to you."

She smirks. "That's a gentle way of saying he threatened my life, right?"

I nod silently. I watch her reaction carefully. She seems calm, taking a deep breath, and before I know what's happening, she crawls into my lap, placing her head in the nook between my neck and shoulder. I instantly wrap my arms around her waist, her gentle hands in mine.

"Do you understand now why I kept everything from you?" I ask her gently. "You're not angry with me for doing that, are you?"

She takes her hands from mine to gently cup my face between them. "Of course I'm not angry, Davison. But I wish you had told me because it's just as important for me to protect you as it is for you to do the same for me."

My heart jumps into my throat.

God, I love this woman so fucking much.

But I'm still anxious for her reply to what I'm going to ask her. I grip her tighter in my arms. "Now you need to tell me something."

"Okay," she whispers.

"Why did you meet with Matteo?"

She lifts her head from my shoulder, her eyes boring directly into mine. "It was totally by chance. He had a job interview in the area and was killing time."

"Did you talk about me?"

She shakes her head, but now smiling, thank God. "Yes, you came up in our conversation."

"Do I need to kick his ass?"

Now she starts laughing for real, cupping my face in her hands. "Oh, my sweet, possessive, territorial boyfriend," she coos. "No ass-kicking will be required because you'll be surprised to hear that he totally picked up on your chest-thumping *Allegra is my woman* caveman vibe back in Italy, so don't worry about that. He gets that and respects it."

I grunt. "Good."

She gives me a quick peck on the lips. "But I'm flattered all the same. Now, tell me what you're going to do about your father."

"I gave him an ultimatum. Either he would report to the Feds of his own volition or I'd do it for him. So far, he hasn't done anything."

"Then you need to talk him into it, Davison," she insists. "He's a bastard for what he did, but he's still your father. You have to help him, as much as it'll kill you to do it."

My Venus—the voice of reason.

"I agree. I'll call my mom and family attorney. I'll ask them to meet me tomorrow at the house so we can all talk to him together and try to get him to come to his senses."

"That sounds like a very good plan," she concurs, leaning in to give me a long kiss, soft and reassuring.

"I'm glad you know everything," I tell her when she pulls her luscious mouth away from me.

She coils her legs around my waist and leans her forehead against mine, holding on to me as if her life depended on it as I grip her tighter, only reinforcing my firm belief that she is my own personal life preserver, unwavering and steadfast. "Me too, Harvard. Me too."

* * *

ALLEGRA

The next morning, I'm lying in bed staring at Davison, who's finally sleeping soundly. He kept me up most of the night, tossing and turning. I know without hesitation what caused him to sleep so poorly—the knowledge that he has to confront his father today, his own parent, to turn himself over to the authorities for his crimes.

He looks so peaceful and beautiful. The stubble on his face sends me reeling with the heady thought of him scratching my inner thighs and pussy with his jaw, stimulating me and hurling me straight into a prolonged orgasm.

Suddenly, he stirs, snapping me out of my fantasy. He flips onto his back and opens his eyes. His head turns to me, those luminous emerald eyes of his making their first appearance of the day, taking me in.

"I love waking up and the first thing I see is you," he says in a raw voice, "with those mesmerizing brown eyes of yours staring back at me. It's the highlight of my day."

I reach out to stroke his jaw, then lay my head down on his hard chest with my face angled so I can look him in the eyes. "Likewise, Harvard. I hope you finally got some decent rest. You were so restless during the night."

His eyebrows furrow in concern. "I didn't keep you up, did I?"

"Don't worry about me. I'm more concerned about you. Are you ready for today?"

"Not really. But I know something that will calm me down."

"Something of an erotic nature?" I joke, my hand traveling south down to his torso.

He grins wickedly at me. "Usually, you'd be right on the money, baby. But no. This time, if you'd be all right with it, I want you to sing for me."

I stop my hand and tilt my head at him curiously. "You never fail to surprise me. And I'd be happy to, because I think I know exactly what you need."

"You always do, Venus."

He smiles at me as I sit up, my knees under me and my hands on top of my thighs. I clear my throat and take a deep breath as I launch into "Musetta's Waltz" from *La Bohème*, an aria I practiced again and again with La Diva.

As I sing the lyrics, I act it out, winking at Davison coquettishly, beckoning to him with my hands, swiveling my shoulders back and forth. And he is totally loving it, judging by the huge, mischievous smile on his face, and the growing bulge I spot under the cotton sheet.

When I finish, he yanks me down to him, clamping his lips over mine as his hot, silky tongue plunges into my mouth.

We kiss and kiss for ages. When we pull apart, he caresses my face, with so much love in his eyes. "Thank you for the distraction, Allegra. That's exactly what I needed."

I softly stroke his strong jaw with my hands. "I wish I could do more for you."

His eyes soften. "Baby, all you ever have to do for me is just be with me and love me."

I smile back at him. "That's easy enough to do."

He pecks me on the cheek. "I'd better get moving. I want to get this over with. You'll wait for me here, right? I want you to be here when I get back."

"There's no place I'd rather be," I reassure him. "Luciana is going to come over and practice with me while I wait for you."

He nods. "Thank you, my love."

I watch as he heads for the bathroom, soaking in the view of his sculpted back and firm ass, listening as the water is turned on in the shower.

My heart is breaking for him. He is the strongest man I know, but I also know how much this is killing him. And because of that, I know my love for Davison Cabot Berkeley will never cease, forever boundless with me.

Chapter Nineteen

DAVISON

Standing outside my father's study, I stare at the faces of my family's attorney, Leonard Preston, and my mother. Leonard nods his head determinedly, while my mother looks at me with worry etched across her face.

I reach for her hand, holding it tightly. "We need to do this, Mom."

"I know," she replies shakily.

I don't even bother to knock, throwing the door open, making my father jump in his desk chair, dropping his cell phone.

"What the hell?" he shouts at us.

"Time's up, Dad," I declare. "We're going to the Feds."

"No chance in hell," he snaps back at me.

I stomp over to his desk, the cherrywood object serving as the barrier from me pummeling my father's face.

"You fucking bastard! Just for once in your life, think of someone other than yourself. What about those pensioners you stole from?"

"I don't give a shit."

"And what about Mom? You care about what happens to her? Your own wife?"

Fire shoots from his eyes at me, but I can't be intimidated by him.

Preston takes a step toward us. "I've been in touch with Malcolm's lawyer, Hart. He's turning himself in, and as your legal counsel, I advise you to do the same. I can only imagine that if you don't, he might implicate you, saying that it was all your idea and you forced him into it."

My father slams his fists on his desk. "He wouldn't do that, Lenny!"

"In my experience, a person will do just about anything to save themselves from prison," he replies knowingly.

Before my father can answer, my mother's voice breaks the silence in the room. "Hartwell, I've been married to you for forty-five years. I've been the dutiful wife. The image of the perfect lady of Manhattan society. You've given me a very good life and a son, who I love with all my heart. I've never questioned anything you've done. But now you have to do what is right. You have to pay for your mistakes. And I will be there in the courtroom with you, sitting right behind you when the judge hands down your prison sentence, still playing my role. You have no choice. For once in your life, it's time to listen to me and your son."

I watch as my father spins his chair away from us, looking out the window. Before Preston, my mother, or I have a chance to repeat our pleas to him, I hear my father mutter, "I'm sorry, Mona."

"Turn around, Hart," my mother asks of him gently.

He doesn't bother to do that, but instead he rises from his chair and walks over to her, taking her hands in his. "I'm so sorry, Mona. For everything. The only reason I hesitated before was because I was worried about my reputation. The reputation of the company. *Our* reputation and social standing."

My mother steps closer to my father. "None of that matters. You're doing what's right. And I'm proud of you." She leans in and takes him in her arms. I don't know how long it's been since I saw my parents exchange any form of affection, and I can't help but warm at the sight of it.

"So," Preston asks trepidatiously, "does this mean you'll give yourself up?"

"Yes, Lenny," he tells him, still holding my mother. "Make all of the arrangements. Just give me as much time as you can so I can be at home with my wife. I promise I won't go anywhere."

"Of course. I'll call my contacts downtown and take care of it."

I exhale in relief. "Thank you, Dad," followed by something that unexpectedly escapes from my mouth before I know I'm even saying it: "I'll come with you when you go to the Feds."

My father turns away from my mother to look at me, a shocked look on his face. "It's all right, Davison. You don't have to do that."

I stare back at him, resolved in my decision. "Yes, Dad. I want to. I need to. For our family."

He stretches out his hand to me. "I don't deserve that, but thank you nonetheless."

I shake it in return. "You're welcome. Just send me the details when you have them. I'm going to go now."

I step over to thank Leonard. Before I walk out, I embrace my mother. "I love you, darling. And thank you," she whispers in my ear.

"I love you too, Mom."

I rush to the front door, anxious for the fresh air outside and something even more than that.

I need Allegra. Right fucking now.

With the Maybach idling in front of the house, I slip into the backseat, Charles already up front at the wheel.

"Get me home, Charles. You see a yellow light, floor it. Understood?"

"Understood, sir."

* * *

When I step out of the elevator, Allegra is waiting for me, dressed in nothing but one of my Harvard T-shirts that hits her just above the knee. I can only imagine what I look like, disheveled and exhausted, but when I stare into her eyes, all I see is the love for me reflected in them. I need her, and I ache for the feel of her in my arms.

She doesn't say a word as she steps toward me, wrapping her arms around me. I dive my head into her silky hair, filling my nose with the sweet scent of her coconut shampoo. I wrap around her, holding on to her like a vise.

"I love you, Allegra. I love you so fucking much," I whisper in her ear. "I don't know what I would do without you."

"That's something you'll never experience, because I will never leave you," she replies to me soothingly in that sweet voice of hers. "I love you too, Davison."

I scoop her up and head for the bedroom, with her arms around my neck, her head nestled on my shoulder. I can hear her hum contentedly, making my dick even harder and my heart threaten to burst out of my chest.

When I reach the bed, I lay her down gently. She sits up and in one swift move, yanks the T-shirt off, immediately lying back down. Her eyes are locked on mine as I undress, leaving all of my clothes in a pile on the floor.

I crawl up the bed to get to her, hovering over her on all fours. I'm hard and desperate to be inside her.

But she has other ideas.

"Fuck my tits, Davison," she commands of me.

I raise my eyebrows at her, both from shock and overwhelming love for this woman, who never fails to surprise me.

With her eyes blazing at me with utter lust, I smirk at her. "Why don't you show me what you have in mind, baby?"

As if I don't know what she meant.

I swear…this woman…fuck if I'm not the luckiest bastard on the planet.

Her steady hands grab my ass, bringing me closer to her. I grip the headboard and kneel on either side of her shoulders. I'm mesmerized by the sight below me as she brings my dick between her two succulent breasts. She clamps it, pushing them together, cushioning and massaging it lodged in the cradle of her soft flesh.

I watch as she lifts her head and starts licking the tip of my cock like a lollipop, swiping off the precum with her tongue.

"Fuck me, you are a goddess, Venus. I can watch you do that for ages," I rasp, barely able to form a coherent sentence because of the erotic scene playing out underneath me by my exquisite girlfriend. She looks up at me, her eyes hooded and her lush pink lips clamped over my dick.

Allegra continues to lick me, but before I know what's happening, she carefully sits up and pushes me down on my back. I don't even have a chance to ask her what she's doing when I feel my cock in her mouth, first licking the veins along the sides, then swallowing me whole, working her mouth up and down, humming as she tastes me wholly.

I reach down to grip her hair, not too tightly but enough to indicate to her that I'm loving every second of what she's doing to me, running my fingers through her silky strands.

My muscles begin to lock as I can sense the release coming, the one that only my Allegra can bring.

"I'm coming…" I shout out to prepare her.

Finally, I roar as I come, spurting into her mouth. When she frees my cock from her mouth, she places her head on my torso, rubbing her chin against my skin to wipe it clean.

I caress her head as she rests after giving me that mind-blowing orgasm. "Gotta tell you, I didn't see that coming at all."

"What can I say? You inspire me, Harvard," I hear her reply.

"And you know you do the same for me, right?"

"I hope so," she whispers.

I'm not happy with the sound of her reply. "Come here to me."

Allegra raises herself, making her way up my body until she reaches my shoulders and I can wrap my arms around her.

"You're the one who pushed me to confront my father because you knew it was the right thing to do. You always make me want to do better, to be better. And nobody has ever had that kind of effect on me."

I lift her chin up so I can see her eyes, wet with unshed tears. "Thank you," she murmurs.

I gently kiss her lips. "You're welcome, baby. Now get on your back so I can reciprocate and fuck you senseless."

She sighs. "If you must..." she teases me in that sexy voice of hers.

I must.

* * *

ALLEGRA

"Thank you, Miss Orsini."

I stare at the panel of judges in the small auditorium that's being used for the regional auditions for the Metropolitan Opera National Council Auditions near Lincoln Center. I sang my go-to aria, "Sì, mi chiamano Mimì" from *La Bohème*. I'd never been so nervous before, probably because I knew how much was riding on this. My graduation recital and even my month with La Diva were so much different in tone and emotion than this. I was never nauseous for either of those. I practically downed an entire liter of ginger ale to calm my nerves before it was my turn to sing.

This is the second day of the auditions. I made it through the first round and was picked for the second to perform in front of a small crowd. I asked only Lucy to come with me because Davison's presence would've attracted too much attention, and he was so busy working with the Berkeley family attorney dealing with the arrangements for the date when his father would turn himself over to the Feds.

I'm now moving into a room where I'm sequestered with the rest of the finalists to await the judges' decision. I know a few of the other finalists from the opera circles that I was introduced to while I was at the conservatory, so we shoot the breeze until someone walks in and tells us the judges have made their decision.

We all wait offstage, pacing the floor, fidgeting with our hands. There are six of us, with one winner who will advance to the semifinals.

Finally, the winners are announced.

I don't win third place. And I don't place second.

"And the winner is…Allegra Orsini!"

I gasp in shock as I feel the others patting my back and one of the volunteers pushing me out. My mouth goes dry as my pulse starts racing. I'm trembling as I make my way onto the stage. When I reach the center, I take a bow and place my hands over my heart, a gesture of thanks to the judges.

There's a reception afterward for the finalists, which I plan to attend, but first, I dash into the audience. Lucy rushes to me to hug me so tightly we can't breathe.

"I'm so proud of you, Alli!" I hear her squeal in my ear.

"I can't believe it! I have to call Davison and Papa, but my purse is backstage."

Lucy reaches into her bag and yanks out her phone, shoving it at me. "Call!"

I punch in Davison's number with shaky fingers. He picks up on the first ring.

"You won, didn't you?" I can hear the smile in his voice.

I want to cry, perceiving the certainty in his voice that I've won and that he knows it's me on the phone and not Lucy. "Yes," I murmur.

"I'm so fucking proud of you, baby," he replies, warming me all over with the love I hear in his voice.

Tears are now flowing freely down my cheeks. "Thank you, Harvard. Listen, I have to go to the reception now, but..."

"Just call me when you're done and I'll come pick you up. I want a quiet night with you tonight," he says softly.

The decrease of the timbre in his voice puts me on alert. "Of course. Anything you want, Harvard."

"I'll see you soon, Venus."

* * *

Two hours later, when I step out of the building where I'd spent most of the day that ended unexpectedly, the first person I see is Davison, standing next to the Maybach, holding a bouquet of a dozen pale apricot roses, my favorites. His eyes are hidden by his black aviator sunglasses, but the wide smile across his face is fully out on display, all for me.

"Congratulations, baby," he greets me with that sexy rumble of his.

I step forward to him, taking the flowers from him and giving him a long, deep kiss, his hands wrapped around my head.

"God, I needed that," I murmur. "I'm so exhausted."

"Come on, let's get you home." He takes me in one hand while opening the car door for me with the other, gently nudging me inside.

Once Charles pulls away from the curb, I crawl over and settle myself in Davison's lap. "Okay, tell me the latest with your father."

He removes his sunglasses and takes a deep breath, exhaling before answering me. "Tomorrow. We're going to the Feds tomorrow."

I nod in understanding. "Do you want me to—"

"Yes," he replies. "I want you to come with me. I need you with me, Allegra."

Yet again, I'm not surprised how natural it was for him to know what I was offering without having to say it. "Of course, Davison. I love you."

He glances down at me, his emerald eyes boring into mine. Then he does something familiar, something that makes my heart race, my pulse quicken, and my pussy begin to moisten with desire.

He pushes the intercom button on the side panel. "Stoplights, Charles."

"Yes, sir."

Davison presses a button to raise the partition between us and the front seat. I straddle his lap as he begins to unbutton my silk blouse, stroking my hardened nipples through my cotton bra.

"I never appreciated the necessity of stoplights until I met you, Davison Cabot Berkeley," I mutter huskily.

"Oh, the things I've yet to teach you, Allegra Orsini," he promises me before clamping his lush lips over mine and plunging his hot, silky tongue in my mouth.

Chapter Twenty

F_{uck!}"

Standing in front of the full-length mirror in my walk-in closet, I look down at the carpeted floor, completely covered in neckties, their labels mocking me from where they're lying on the ground.

I can't focus.

I can't focus because I'm preparing to help my father surrender to federal authorities for running a bogus scam and bilking senior citizens out of their life savings.

I can't find the right tie to go with my suit. My decision-making capabilities are fried from the events of the last few days.

I don't even notice Allegra next to me until she gently places her hand on my shoulder. "Let me help you, Davison," she whispers in a soft but firm voice.

She glances down at the floor around my feet. "Yellow stands out too much, red is too brazen, and gray is too dull," she comments. "You need an understated color that won't overwhelm, yet something that will display your strength."

Her eyes roam over me as she takes in my blue suit, then moves to the tie rack and begins shuffling through them, finally pulling out the perfect one, which I completely disregarded—a dark blue Armani tie that matches my jacket and trousers but contrasts against my pale shirt.

She hangs it around my neck and under the collar, allowing me to finish the task, using her beautiful long fingers to tighten it in the hollow of my collarbone and smoothing it out.

"There," she says, stepping back to admire her work. "That'll do."

I stare into the mirror. She's right, of course. Now I can face the Feds.

She turns my chin so she can look into my eyes. "It'll be okay. I'll be with you the entire time."

She's in a cream dress with a black lace collar, the same one that she wore when she went to my parents' house for the first time. My heart swells inside my chest with my love for her and the eternal gratitude I'll always hold for her coming into my life.

I lean in and give her a long kiss. "Thank you, baby." I glance at my watch. "We'd better go."

Taking her hand, I lead us out of the bedroom, grabbing my phone and wallet on the way out. We don't say a word to each other until we get into the Maybach.

The building that holds the federal offices where we're meeting my father is less than a five-minute drive from my apartment near the World Financial Center. When we pull up, only our family attorney is waiting for us outside.

I get the door for Allegra as I usually do, then join her and Leonard Preston on the sidewalk.

"Malcolm Canterbury is already inside with his wife and daughter," he informs us. "Your father called that he and your mother will be here shortly."

Just as I nod to acknowledge him, I spot my parents' black Mercedes sedan pulling up to the curb.

Their driver steps out to open the door for them. My mother is dressed in one of her Chanel suits, and my dad looks somber in a dark gray Armani three-piece.

My mother kisses both Allegra and me on the cheek, while my dad simply addresses us by our names with a quick nod.

"Good, we're all here. Let's go in," Preston declares authoritatively in an attempt to move us along.

I grab Allegra's hand and join the others as we start to walk toward the entrance of the building when I hear a loud pop ring out. Before I can comprehend what's happening, my father falls to the ground, the dark gray of his suit jacket covered in red from the blood gushing out of him.

"Get down!" I shout, falling on top of Allegra, watching as Preston does the same to shield my mother.

Just as I push Allegra down on the concrete, I hear another shot, then a burning pain shoots through my left shoulder. I scream out in agony. I can hear her shouting my name when I sense someone's hands on my right shoulder, wrenching me off her and turning me over. The pain in my shoulder is unbearable and I know that I'm about to pass out. As I swivel my head back and forth, in my field of vision, I spot a man in a blue shirt yelling into a walkie-talkie, and similarly dressed men are running everywhere, guns drawn.

But the only voice I want to hear now is Allegra's, and she's yelling my name, holding my hand and pressing on my open wound, looking into my eyes, telling me to stay with her…and I want to…God, I want to…but my eyes are closing…The ache is too much.

"Can you hear me, Davison?" she shouts. "Don't you fucking leave me! I love you!"

"Love you, baby…" I whisper before everything goes dark.

Chapter Twenty-One

The irony of where I'm sitting now is a joke. A very bitter, evil, cruel joke.

I'm in a private waiting room on the surgical floor of NewYork-Presbyterian Hospital, but at their downtown location in Lower Manhattan.

It was only a few months ago when I was a patient at the one on the Upper East Side after I'd fallen down the stairs at Davison's parents' house during the benefit for the conservatory. And now, Davison is the patient, being operated on to remove the bullet lodged inside his left shoulder.

If I dared to laugh from the irony, it wouldn't be a funny ha-ha type of laugh, but more of an *Are you fucking kidding me?* one, taking the Lord's name in vain in a continuous rant.

Holding one of Mrs. Berkeley's hands, I stare down at the crumpled towelette gripped in my other one. One of the nurses gave it to me to wipe off Davison's blood, but most of it is still under my fingernails, dark and dried. I smile slightly, imagining it as a twisted metaphor for him and how he's gotten under my skin.

When I look over at Davison's mother, our appearances match in an absurd, macabre fashion. Our knees and hands both have scrapes on them from when we were pushed down to the concrete, all of which were tended to by the same nurse who gave me the antiseptic wipe. The clothes we're wearing are torn, with the tips of our shoes scuffed. We sit quietly, not saying a word, undoubtedly doing the same thing—praying for our men to make it through their surgeries.

The only sound in the room is the voice of Leonard Preston, who's been on his phone non-stop since we were ushered in here a few hours ago. And I'm actually grateful for it because silence would be too oppressive.

But I can't stop the movie in my head that's playing on a continuous loop—

I hit the pavement with a hard thud. *Davison's solid, muscled body protects me like a shield of armor when suddenly he screams in my ear and his body goes limp.*

"Davison, what is it? Talk to me!"

Someone is pulling him off me, and when I sit up, I see his left shoulder covered in blood, his face and lips gone pale.

"Oh my God! Davison!" I scream.

I crawl over to him, turning his head to me. His eyes are fluttering and unfocused.

"Davison! Stay with me!" I beg. I hold one of his hands, us-

ing the other to put pressure on his shoulder. "Can you hear me? Don't you fucking leave me!"

I know policemen are scurrying around, guns drawn, scouring rooftops, yelling instructions to one another, but I'm not giving them my full attention because the man I love is lying on cold pavement, bleeding out from a gunshot wound.

I release his hand to use both of mine to bear down on his wound because his blood is now gushing out, and until EMS gets here, I'm not letting go.

"I love you!" I shout, an unspoken plea for him not to close his eyes.

Suddenly, I hear him whisper, "Love you, baby," and when I glance over at him, his eyes are closing.

I gasp in shock, my heart plummeting like a boulder into my torso, and my chest fills with the purest form of fear, even worse than what I experienced when that scum Carlo Morandi kidnapped me. A million times worse.

I grip Davison's beautiful face with my hands, covered in his blood, shaking it slightly, willing him to open his emerald eyes.

"Open your eyes, Davison!" I beg. "Please!"

A large hand settles on my shoulder. "Ma'am, step aside, please. We've got it."

When I turn around, two paramedics are setting their equipment on the ground, ready to help Davison.

I sit back, watching the two men in EMS uniforms work on Davison, unable to move, hoping to hear his deep voice again.

"Miss Orsini?"

I look up and see Mr. Preston hovering over me. "Are you all right?"

I'm so tempted to snap at him, What do you think? I'm not the one with a bullet in my shoulder, idiot! *But I simply reply,* "Yes, I'm fine," *not taking my eyes from Davison.*

"Mrs. Berkeley went in the ambulance with her husband. You can come with me in my car."

"No, I'm going with Davison," *I reply firmly.*

"I don't think—"

"I'm going with him!" *I shout back, watching as Davison is lifted onto the stretcher.*

"That's fine," *I hear him answer me.* "I'll meet you at the hospital."

I jump to my feet, grabbing my purse, following the paramedics wheeling Davison to the waiting ambulance. I wait until he's hauled inside, then jump in right behind him.

We take off, sirens wailing. I sit back in a corner, staying out of the way so the paramedics can work on Davison and keep him alive.

I'm going to ask, but I'm so afraid of the answer.

"Is he going to be okay?"

"We're doing everything we can, ma'am," *one of them replies, which sounds like a standard, noncommittal answer to me.*

I clasp my hands together, taking deep breaths and not allowing my gaze to stray from Davison. I take in his strong jaw, the lush shape of his lips, the silky strands of his dark hair. I can't reach out to hold his hand, with one of the paramedics blocking my path.

I repeat the same thing internally: Hang on, Davison. Don't leave me. I need you. I love you.

My prayer is interrupted by the ambulance coming to a sudden stop. The doors are thrown open. The gurney that has the love of my life strapped to it is unlocked and pulled out. I rush out, running right on the heels of the medical team that's wheeling him toward an elevator.

A hand grabs my arm. "Come with me, Miss Orsini." *A woman in a red suit with an ID badge pinned to her jacket identifying her as JULIA KENYON–ADMINISTRATION is standing next to me, her face warm and comforting.* "I'll take you to the surgical floor. Mrs. Berkeley is already there."

Riding up in the elevator, she does all of the talking. "I've secured a private waiting room for you and Mrs. Berkeley in light of the situation…"

She keeps on talking, but it's all white noise to me. I just want to see Davison.

When I walk through the door of the waiting room, Mrs. Berkeley rises from her chair, looks at my face, and bursts into tears. I rush into her arms as we embrace and cry together, united in our agony and fear.

The sound of the door opening snaps my mind back to the present. Two tall, balding men in nondescript suits walk in, revealing police badges from their breast pockets.

"Mrs. Berkeley? I'm Detective Wallace, and this is my partner, Detective McDougal. We need to ask you about the shootings."

Preston steps forward. "Gentlemen, I'm Leonard Preston, the Berkeley family attorney. This is a very difficult time. Can't this wait?"

"We just have a few routine questions, sir. Can you quickly tell us what happened?"

Davison's mother nods and clears her throat. "We were all walking toward the building when someone shot my husband from the back. Then Leonard pushed me to the ground and I saw my son do the same to Allegra. And then he was shot. Does that answer your question?"

"Why were you going to the federal building?"

"That is a personal matter between my client and the authorities," Preston replies, putting a stop authoritatively to that line of questioning.

I need to know something. "Have you caught the shooter?"

The two cops shift their gazes at me. "And you are?" one of them asks.

"She is Allegra Orsini, my son's girlfriend, and I'd like to know the answer to that as well," Mrs. Berkeley demands.

"Not yet, ma'am. We're reviewing the footage from the CCTV cameras now," Detective McDougal says, which doesn't bring me any comfort. "Do you know of anyone who would want to harm your husband or son?"

"Again, Detective," Preston interrupts, "that has to do with the federal case. If you want more information about that, you'll have to ask them."

Before the detectives can ask another question, a doctor dressed in green scrubs walks into the room. He is tall with salt-and-pepper hair, exuding an air of confidence. My heart leaps at the sight of him because he doesn't appear stressed or overwhelmed, all of which I hope are positive signs.

Davison's mother and I jump from our chairs at the same time, gripping our hands tightly.

"Excuse me, I'm Dr. Bradford Chapin, chief of surgery. Mrs. Berkeley?" he asks.

"I'm Mona Cabot Berkeley," she declares. "How are my husband and son?"

"They're both fine…"

We both start to cry from relief at the sound of those three words.

"We removed the bullet from your son's shoulder. He suffered no major internal injuries."

"Thank God," I whisper.

"Your husband's case was trickier because of the location of the bullet around his intestinal system, but I managed to get it out without causing any further damage. He's very lucky that his spine wasn't affected."

Mrs. Berkeley nods her head in understanding. "When can we see them?"

"They're in recovery now," Dr. Chapin replies. "Only one person per patient. Family only."

The next words out of her mouth both stun and warm me at the sound of them. "Allegra *is* family," she informs him. "Take us to them."

"Of course, Mrs. Berkeley. This way," he says, holding the door open for us.

With our hands still clamped together, we follow Dr. Chapin down the hallway. "Allegra, you go to Davison. I'll be with Hart."

"Okay," I barely manage.

The doctor leads us to a room where a policeman is standing guard. He pushes the door open for us. A curtain is pulled to separate the two beds in the room. I look over at Mr. Berkeley, pale and silent in his bed.

Together, Davison's mother and I stop to take in his appearance. My pulse starts to race, anxious to see Davison, worried about what he'll look like. She tugs on my hand, pulling me forward. We come around the curtain.

I gasp at the sight of Davison, surrounded by beeping machines and tubes hanging from his arms. His face is pale, his beautiful green eyes shut. His left shoulder is covered in white gauze and bandages.

I watch as his mother walks up to him and kisses him on the forehead. She pulls up a chair to his bedside, close enough so I can hold his hand. "Come and sit down, dear. I'll be with Hart."

She gives me one last hug before she disappears behind the curtain. I slowly make my way to the chair and settle in. I take his strong hand in mine, kissing his knuckles, stroking it against my cheek.

I need him to know I'm here. Still holding his hand, I stand up and lean closer to him so I can talk into his ear.

"Hi, Harvard. It's me. Allegra. I'm here. And you're going to be okay. Just open your eyes as soon as you can because I want you back with me, teasing me and laughing with me and driving me crazy. I love you, Davison. Just open your eyes."

I shut my eyes, pressing his hand to my lips.

Fuck, Davison. Just open them, okay? Please. I can't lose you now.

* * *

DAVISON

Coconut.
 I smell coconut.
 Allegra.
 I need to see her.
I pry my eyes open, rewarded by the sight of her standing over me, her dark brown eyes locked on mine, but they're reddened, breaking my heart when I see them in that state. But then I'm rewarded when a huge smile overtakes her glorious face when she sees I'm awake.

"Oh my God! Davison! Thank God!" she cries out, tears flowing down her soft cheeks. She kisses my hand, holding it to her face.

I test out my voice to see if it's working. "Allegra," I manage, but very roughly.

She starts to cry even harder, leaning in to kiss my face over and over. I try to reciprocate, but I start coughing persistently. "Water."

"Of course. Just a second."

She reaches for a pitcher on the bedside table, pouring water into the cup sitting next to it, shoving a straw in before she holds it up to my mouth. She pokes the straw gently between my lips. I suck on it, the cool liquid running down my dry throat, hydrating my parched mouth.

I finish every last drop of the water, the straw sucking the bottom of the cup.

"More?"

I hand the cup back to her. "I'm good, baby."

With her back to me, I hear her sniffle as she puts the cup back on the table.

God, I love her.

I'm not a religious man, but I'm so grateful to whatever higher power that decided I was worthy enough to stay on this mortal coil and live the rest of my life with this beautiful, selfless woman.

"Hey, get over here, Venus," I order her, my voice sounding stronger now.

When Allegra turns around, she's busy trying to wipe away the fresh tears that are forming in her eyes.

I pat the space next to me on the bed. She grins and steps over to me, sitting down by my side.

I take her hand and squeeze it hard to reassure her. "I'm here and I'm okay, so stop with the waterworks, got it?"

She laughs sweetly, a sound I thought I'd never hear again. "I'm sorry. Hearing you call me 'baby' and 'Venus' again and bossing me around…it just…it's music to my fucking ears, okay?"

"Ah, now, that's music to my ears, hearing that filthy word coming from your luscious mouth."

We stare at each other for a long minute, and then my mind starts recalling everything. "How is my father?"

"He's fine. He's actually lying on a bed right behind that curtain," she informs me, gesturing to her right.

Wasn't expecting that. "Really? Do we know yet who shot us?"

"No, Harvard, not yet."

I smile at the sound of her endearing nickname for me, which

I never get tired of hearing. Suddenly, I yawn, fatigue creeping in.

"I'm falling asleep, baby. You should go get some rest."

She sighs resignedly. "Okay, I'll stay until you fall asleep. But I'll kiss you before I go."

"Oh yes, I absolutely insist," I smirk.

She places her soft lips on mine, plunging her tongue into my mouth. We don't rush, savoring the familiar taste of each other.

When she pulls back, she gives me one last quick kiss. "I love you, Davison. I'll be back soon."

I caress her cheek with my index finger. "I love you too, Allegra."

As I close my eyes, I can hear her humming in my ear, then singing the lyrics to "The Sweetest Taboo," one of the Sade songs that she put on my iPod before she left for Italy. Her angelic voice lulls me to sleep contentedly, knowing I'm still alive and that my Allegra is with me.

Chapter Twenty-Two

The next morning when I walk into Davison's hospital room, his father's bed is empty. I hear two male voices talking behind the curtain. When I step around it, the same detectives who questioned his mother and me yesterday are doing the same to Davison.

I look at him, and I know his joyous smile mirrors the one that I'm wearing now on my face. His emerald eyes light up at my appearance, and his face looks less pale than last night.

Dressed in a beige hospital gown, with his gorgeous face full of scruff, I'm convinced he can make anything look sexy as hell on him.

"Gentlemen, we're going to have to end your questions for now because I have something more important to do at this moment," he informs them. "I need to kiss my girlfriend."

I blush slightly at his direct words. Without having to say anything more, I walk up to him and kiss him soundly on the mouth. I can hear the detectives coughing and tittering awkwardly, but we honestly couldn't care less. Davison was almost taken away from me, and if our public display of affection bothers someone, so be it.

"Yes, umm, of course, Mr. Berkeley. We'll be in touch," one of the men announces.

He pulls back from me. "Thank you, detectives. Good day," he tells them, not removing his eyes from mine.

"Morning, baby." He strokes my face with the pads of his thumbs.

"Good morning, Harvard. Did they have anything new to report?"

"Yeah, they got footage of the shooter off the security cameras. He's the same guy who confronted me outside my building. Apparently, he's a gun for hire. I'm guessing my father's partners in Chicago hired him to kill my father before he could turn himself in."

"But why would they try to hurt you?"

"Who knows. It's just a matter of time before they find him."

I sit down in the chair next to his bed. "Thank God for that."

Davison's eyebrows furrow confusedly. "Hey, where do you think you're going?"

"What?"

"Come closer."

I pull the chair right up to his bed.

He shakes his head. "Closer."

I roll my eyes and sit down on the open space next to him on the mattress.

I laugh when he opens up the space next to his right arm, indicating what he really wants me to do. "I'm the patient. You have to see to my needs, Nurse Orsini."

I kick off my sandals and curl in beside him. He instantly wraps his arm around my waist. "Ah, much better," he sighs, kissing my hair.

"Where's your dad?" I ask.

"Having tests. It's been quite an experience sharing a room with him. He snores like a fucking buzz saw."

I laugh. "I'll take your word for it."

The curtain flutters, and Dr. Chapin, the one who operated on Davison, appears in front of us, this time in his white lab coat.

"Good morning, Mr. Berkeley. How are you feeling?"

"Fine. Ready to go home. How soon will that happen, Doc?"

I can tell from the frown on Dr. Chapin's face he's not used to being addressed so casually or seeing a patient's girlfriend lying in the same bed as the patient.

"You need to heal, Mr. Berkeley," he admonishes us, not so passive-aggressively.

Davison hugs me tighter and kisses my forehead. "Allegra is the only cure I need, Doctor Chapin."

"Yes, well, just take it easy." He huffs. "Once all of your tests are clear, you should be released in the next twenty-four hours."

"That's exactly what I needed to hear. Thanks, Doc."

Dr. Chapin nods. "I'll check on you later," he mutters, leaving as quickly as he entered.

Once we hear the door shut firmly, I dissolve into laughter, burying my head in his right shoulder. "Oh my God! What is it with you today? Is it your goal to embarrass me in front of everyone you come into contact with?"

He laughs in return. "No, that's just a bonus."

I shake my head amusedly. "If I'll be seeing to your needs, should I purchase a nurse's uniform?"

"No, that won't be necessary," he says with a straight face, "since you'll be naked the entire time during my convalescence back at my apartment."

"Christ, you're impossible," I sigh, dropping my head on his healthy shoulder.

A few silent minutes pass between us when a realization strikes me.

"Oh my God…"

"What's wrong, baby?" he asks, his voice raised in concern.

I grip his body tighter. "Remember when I went to see Ashton to ask if she knew anything about what was going on with you?"

He grunts in acknowledgment. "Yes. What about it?"

"Before I left, she said she didn't know until that moment how much I really loved you…"

"And?"

"I told…I told her that I'd take a bullet for you."

I start to cry, and Davison holds me closer to him. "Oh, Allegra, please don't cry. Do you feel guilty that what you said came true and you couldn't protect me?"

He knows me so damn well.

I nod through my tears.

"Well, don't. That's crazy. None of us knew that was going to happen, so stop with the tears, got it?" he pleads with me.

"Okay," I acquiesce, wiping my eyes with my fingers.

"Look at me, baby," he asks softly.

I shift my eyes to his. He stares back at me tenderly. "I'm shatterproof. We both are. You're stuck with me, Orsini. For better or worse."

"I wouldn't mind more of the better from this point on."

"Too right, Venus. Now kiss me."

My smile stretches across my face as I lean in to kiss him. His mouth is warm and comforting as his tongue tangles with mine, and I revel in the taste of him.

When I pull away, he lays his head back and shuts his eyes, while I rest my head between his hard pecs so I can listen to his heartbeat, grateful for the strong, steady sound of it, pumping away in his broad, muscled chest.

He is still here. With me.

Chapter Twenty-Three

DAVISON

I'm not going to lie. I grew up in a very privileged manner. I attended private schools and the finest university in the world. I spent my summer vacations at our family chalet in Switzerland. There was nothing that couldn't be had with a swipe of a credit card or bank transfer. I rarely heard the word "no."

But as I sit at my dining room table one week later after being released from the hospital watching Leonard Preston complete final negotiations of my father's surrender and penalty with the two federal agents across from him, I realize the trappings I grew up with are worthless. They are things that could've been taken away just like that. And everything that my father ever taught me was based on lies and shallow morals.

As the last points are made and confirmed, I think of how the one good thing in my life, the only thing of worth, is in my bedroom right now, sleeping peacefully after our marathon night of smoking-hot sex. Ever since I got home from the hospital, we've been beasts with each other, partly because of the thought that we came so close to losing each other again and also because, well, my Venus is a fucking goddess and I can't keep my hands off her. We've had to be careful at times because my shoulder is still healing, but we work around my injury. We're very considerate and accommodating of one another, but nothing will ever keep us from fucking until we're both spent and sated.

"If that's it, gentlemen, I'll show you out," Preston says commandingly. "My client will turn himself over tomorrow. We'll be at your offices at nine a.m."

I stand from my chair and escort the three men out. Once the elevator doors shut behind them, I fall back against the wall, exhaling deeply.

"Are they gone?" a sweet voice asks from the kitchen.

I turn and smile at the sound that I want to hear for the rest of my life.

"Yes, baby."

I walk toward Allegra, wrapping her tightly in my arms. I inhale her wet hair, intoxicated by the familiar coconut scent.

"How did it go?"

"Come with me. I'll tell you everything."

I take her by the hand and lead her to the living room sofa. I sit down first, then settle her comfortably on my lap.

"Dominic will be spending the rest of his life behind the walls of a prison cell for his crimes. We still don't know who sent Ian that prospectus letter, but I think it might've been Dominic's assistant, since Dominic was a total asshole to work for. My dad and Ashton's father will have to do some time as well, but minimum security. The Feds were more lenient with them since they were going to turn themselves in. No supermax prison for Hartwell Berkeley and Malcolm Canterbury. And, of course, there are the financial penalties."

"Meaning what?"

"The Feds are seizing the house in Sutton Square and the chalet in Gstaad. And the company will become insolvent."

She gently loops her arms around my neck, nuzzling my cheek with her nose. "I'm so sorry, Davison. I know how much that company meant to you. It's your family legacy. You're the strongest man I've ever met, but this must be killing you."

I've never been more grateful for this woman than I am at this very moment.

"I thought I'd pass it on to my son one day," I confess wistfully. "My great-grandfather built the company from nothing. He had a miserable childhood, so he came over from England in the late eighteen hundreds to explore America and decided to stay."

"That's him in the portrait in your office, right?"

I smile slightly. "I can't believe you remember that. Yes, that's him. Mason Hartwell Berkeley. And now it's gone."

"What about your mother?"

"She's going to stay in Europe for a while until the media circus dies down. She hasn't decided yet on London or Paris. Once she decides to come back, I'll find an apartment for her."

"Davison, what are you going to do now?" she asks softly.

I tilt her head so I can look into her warm brown eyes. "Don't worry about me, baby. I'm already thinking ahead. The wheels are turning."

"Do you mean you're going to start your own company?"

"Something like that," I hint with a smile.

"I don't know much about business, but if there's any way I can help—"

I cut her off with a hard kiss. "That is how you help me the most."

She laughs aloud. "That's easy enough." She pulls herself off my lap. "How about a late breakfast? I'm starving."

"You start without me. I'll be right there."

"Don't take too long," she calls over her shoulder as she makes her way back to the kitchen.

Once I hear her puttering around, opening and shutting cabinets, I sit back on the couch, smiling to myself.

She thinks I was talking about business when I said I was already thinking ahead.

Good. Then she has no idea what I have planned for her.

* * *

ALLEGRA

"Are you coming or not?"

"Will you cool your jets, Harvard?"

"I swear to God, woman, if you don't get out here in the next five seconds, I'm opening this without you."

"Davison, so help me if I hear the sound of tearing paper out there, no sex for you tonight, buddy boy!"

I hear him groan in frustration in his living room, making me smile wickedly. I step over to the floor-length mirror to check myself out. Everything is in place.

I walk over to the bedroom door. "Okay, now!" I shout out to him down the hallway.

I hear the rustle of tearing paper, and then, "No fucking way!" coming from Davison.

That's my cue.

With the greatest of pain, I strut down the hallway to the living room in the six-inch knee-high leather boots that Lucy insisted I get to match the rest of my outfit.

Davison doesn't see me right away because his back is to me and he's studying the gift I gave him—a karaoke machine. I cough to gain his attention.

He starts turning around to face me. "You are too—"

At the sight of me, his eyes widen like saucers and his mouth drops. Exactly the reaction I was hoping for.

I smirk as I watch his fiery eyes roam over my body, taking in my attire—the leather bustier that's pushing my boobs together, the tight leather miniskirt that hits me at midthigh, and the fishnet stockings that cover my legs, all in black. Then, he focuses on my face—the liquid black liner drawn on my eyes, the smoky eye shadow, and cherry-red lipstick painted onto my lips. With my hair properly moussed and tousled, I'm transformed from a classically trained opera singer into a rock-and-roll sexpot, and I'm about to disprove a point Davison made back in the villa in Lake Como. Now that it's been two weeks since he's been home from the hospital, I decided the time was right for his surprise.

"Fuck, baby…" he murmurs under his breath.

"That'll come later," I purr. "You like?"

"Are you kidding, Venus? You are giving me such a hard-on right now. Why don't you come over to see for yourself?" he asks enticingly.

"Later, Harvard. Right now, why don't you use that Ivy League–educated brain of yours to set that thing up?" I command, gesturing to the machine. "I'm going to give you a special private performance."

In a heartbeat, he's prying the box open with his bare hands. I grab a knife from the kitchen to help him out, handing it to him handle first. I hold the box as he pulls out the machine.

While he plugs it into the wall and quickly skims the instructions, I grab a CD that I left on the kitchen counter. I walk back into the living room and insert it into the machine, searching for the right song, and then hitting "play."

"Have a seat, Berkeley," I command him, pointing to the love seat instead of the couch so nothing is obstructing my path to him.

I take the microphone in hand as the opening sounds of an electric guitar fill the room as I start to sing the opening notes to "Bad Reputation."

Davison laughs out loud at me singing along with Joan Jett. As much as I'm trying to maintain the hard rocker persona, I'm trying to suppress the giggles that are attempting to divert me from my intentions of trying to prove to him that I can sing rock music, but also, to let him see a side of me that he's never seen before because this is just not me. Even though I can tell the karaoke machine isn't of the best quality, I'm having too much fun now, shaking my hair and swiveling my hips, making sure he's keeping his eyes on me by pointing at him with my index finger, then at myself when the lyric calls for it.

The song ends with a burst of defiance, and I'm left standing with my breath panting, my face covered in perspiration, mostly from the pain of having my boobs bound together by the constricting leather.

Davison jumps to his feet and screams, "Yeah, baby!" with his arms raised into the air. He pulls me to him and hauls me into his arms, his hands on my ass, twirling me around as we both laugh aloud from astonishment and the pure joy of being together.

He finally releases me and sets me on the floor. "That was payback for Como, wasn't it?"

"Not so much payback," I counter. "Just wanted to prove a point."

He slowly runs a finger over the tops of my breasts. "You're always going to keep me on my toes, aren't you?" he whispers.

The shift of the tone in his voice throws me off. "I hope so," I reply nervously, shivering at his touch, not completely sure where he's going with this.

"Have a seat, Allegra," he tells me, pushing me gently back onto the love seat. "I'll be right back."

My eyebrows furrow with concern as I watch him walk down the hallway, then return with three small boxes, two square and one narrow and rectangular.

He hands me the narrow one. "I want you to open this one first."

"Davison, this is too much," I mutter under my breath.

"Nothing is ever too much for you, Venus," he replies with a serious look across his face.

The box lies heavily in my lap as I untie the ribbon around the box and sift through the tissue paper. The cover of a book reveals itself to me, the title written in both Italian and English—"An Erotic History of Italy."

I dissolve into laughter. "Oh my God! Is this how you found out about the places in Italy where we stayed? The palazzo in Venice and the villa in Lake Como?"

He smirks. "Yup. Now open the cover and look at the upper right-hand corner."

I do as he says, and my mouth drops in shock, tears instantly forming in my eyes.

My mother's signature—"Concetta Rossetti"—is scrawled across the top, written in her beautiful cursive penmanship.

I can't look at Davison because I'm still too overcome by emotion, tears streaming down my cheeks. "Where did you get this?"

He sits down next to me, joining me on the loveseat. "When we first started dating, I asked your father to lend me some books about learning Italian, the culture of Italy, those kinds of things. He gave this one to me inadvertently, and when I pointed it out to him, he said I could keep it so I could give it to you one day."

I smile. "Smart. I don't think I could've handled having Papa give this to me as a gift, considering the subject matter."

"Exactly," he concurs.

I wipe my eyes, then lean in and kiss Davison softly on the lips. "Thank you. This means the world to me."

"You're welcome, baby, but we're not done yet."

He stands up and reaches for the next box, placing it in my lap. "One down, two to go."

I sigh amusedly as I open it to reveal a black velvet ring box, the very one that Davison had presented to me before I left for Italy with the key to his apartment inside it.

I start to cry again when I open it, the key staring back at me.

"Will you, Allegra?" he asks.

I look up at him. My reply mirrors his question in its tender simplicity. "Yes."

I jump from the seat into his arms, kissing him firmly, wrapping my arms around him tightly, never wanting to let go.

Then he unexpectedly uncoils my arms from his neck. "You need to be sitting down for the last one," he declares, pushing me back into the love seat.

"Whatever you say, Mr. Bossy," I reply, rolling my eyes, giving him an amused smile.

When he hands me the last box, I shake it just to bring some levity to the moment.

"Be careful," he warns me sternly. When I glance at him, he seems anxious.

He's unnerving me. "Are you all right?"

He takes a deep breath. "Never better, baby," he replies confidently, all of his nervousness dissipated.

Okaaaay…

Under the thin layer of tissue, my hand comes into contact with another small box. Its corners have slanted edges, which raises my curiosity. I look up at Davison, who is staring back at me, his eyes dark and serious.

"Go on," he commands in the low rumble of his voice that arouses me to my core.

I finally pull back the tissue to see what is hiding under it. I gasp, my hand flying to my mouth to cover it, stunned beyond belief.

It's the Cartier ring box, the box that Ashton had told me held her newly purchased engagement ring from Davison, but which actually turned out to be an antique ring that had belonged to his grandmother and was never intended for Ashton.

And now…my hands are shaking from the mere thought of what's about to happen.

Davison drops to one khaki-clad knee, taking my hand to turn it over so he can place the red Cartier box on my palm.

"Open it, Allegra," he manages, his voice breaking from the heady feeling of this life-changing moment.

I press the gold button on the bottom of the box, revealing the stunning diamond ring inside it.

Through my blurred vision because of the tears that are now freely running down my face, I can see Davison take the ring and place it on the appropriate finger of my left hand.

"Oh my God, it's so beautiful," I murmur, barely able to speak, my throat choked up from the emotion pulsing throughout my body, my hands shaking in anticipation.

"Allegra Orsini, from the moment my eyes met yours that night at Le Bistro, I knew I was going to marry you—"

"You did not," I mutter, shocking myself and Davison for breaking the moment.

I clamp my right hand over my mouth in disbelief, but then just as quickly, we both laugh, slightly lessening the weight of what's happening but not taking away the joy of it.

Davison shakes his head and smiles, taking my hand, and caresses his thumb over it, just like that first night we met.

"And that, my Venus, is why I'm doing this. Why I'm asking you to spend the rest of your life with me. You love me for who I am. You never cease to surprise me. You're never afraid to tell me when I'm being an ass, but you're always there for me when I need you. I want to be a better man because of you. You make me laugh until it hurts. And I want to be your constant, like you are for me, so you will know that I will always support you, no matter where your career takes you. I want to be there for your ups and downs. We've been through so much, all of which taught me that I want your face to be the first thing I see in the morning and the last thing when I lay my head down at night."

I'm now fully crying. It's the ugly cry, and with Davison's eyes turning moist, it's just getting worse. But I keep as still as I possibly can...

"I love you, Allegra. Will you marry me?"

I nod my head so hard that it starts to hurt, but I don't care. "Yes, yes, of course I'll marry you!"

I slide from my seat to the floor on my knees to join Davison, tackling him as I collapse on top of him. Our mouths find each other, kissing each other in pure, unmitigated happiness, knowing that we are going to be together for the rest of our lives. The security of that knowledge suddenly heightens my need for him. I want to give everything of myself to him, to show him the gratitude I have for him coming into my life and the love for him that has only grown with time, all of the things that words cannot adequately express.

I jump up from the floor as Davison's eyes widen confusedly. "What the—"

When he sees me unhooking the bustier and undoing my skirt, he only says one word to me in a low, raw timbre that moistens my pussy: "Hurry."

An audible groan escapes his mouth when I'm left naked, except for my stockings, garter belt, and the stiletto boots. I carefully step over until I'm standing over him, one foot on either side of his head, my pussy bare and on display for him as I watch him below and await his next command.

"Pussy. Now…" he grunts.

I obey him, easing my knees down to the floor. His strong, firm hands grab my ass as I'm pushed forward, my palms flat on the carpet to steady myself.

I hear him inhale my scent, and then he devours me wholly with his mouth and tongue, sucking and licking and nipping, sending me spiraling until I think I'm going to pass out from his ministrations. He takes all of me, moaning and groaning as he feasts on me like a wild beast. It is pure fucking ecstasy.

"Oh God, Davison…yes! Fuck yes!" I scream, unraveling with every second of his mouth eating me out.

My body begins to shudder. I dig my hands into the fibers of the carpet, bearing down on them to keep me aloft so Davison can finish his meal. The heat from the carpet fabric begins to burn my skin as I finally shout out in release, my cream gushing out over his mouth and chin.

I try to keep myself upright, but before I can steady myself, Davison whips me up and onto my back. His mouth dives onto mine as we kiss each other hard, our teeth knocking together. I taste myself on him, wanting to absorb every last taste of me from his mouth that's combined with his.

Suddenly, he pulls back. "Lock those fucking boots around my waist, baby," he growls at me.

I do as he asks, and in an instant, he plunges his cock inside me, swollen and hard as steel. He thrusts into me again and again, our skin slapping together and our raw groans the only sounds in the room. My fingernails dig into his rock-hard ass, pushing him farther into me, telling him silently to go harder and faster. He obeys, increasing his speed as his shaft pummels me. He's never fucked me like this, our bodies in total sync, and I don't ever want him to stop.

With my head thrown back, I hear him command, "Look at me, baby," and when I do, he pinches my clit, sending me reeling with my back arching and screaming his name from my lips in sacred worship.

He finally falls from utter exhaustion to the floor next to me. He scoops my head with one hand, cradling it while the other collapses like a boulder onto my chest, heavy and sated.

Our panting breaths echo in the wide space. I gain enough strength to turn my head to his, our eyes softened from our mutual release.

"I just have one thing to say to you, future Mrs. Davison Cabot Berkeley," he rasps.

I smile. "What?"

"We're keeping the karaoke machine."

Chapter Twenty-Four

DAVISON

Six months later…

Leaning my elbows on the edge of my family's private box at the Met, I hold my hands clasped together pressed to my mouth as if in prayer with shivers running up and down my body, listening in awe to the lyrical voice that is booming off the acoustics right now in this iconic space.

My fiancée, Allegra Orsini, is onstage, performing her second aria of the afternoon at the Grand Finals Concert of the Metropolitan Opera National Council Auditions. She is singing her beloved "Sì, mi chiamano Mimi." Dressed in a one-shouldered black gown that accentuates her curves to perfection with her hair pulled back into the low chignon that she prefers, she is a vision of beauty that lifts my heart to the fucking rafters because she is mine.

The aria comes to an end. Suddenly, the audience erupts into cheers of "*Brava!*" I jump to my feet to shout out for her, as do the rest of the occupants of the box—Allegra's father; Luciana and Tomas; and Allegra's two mentors, Signora Pavoni and La Diva, who flew in from Milan specifically to see her apprentice perform on the Met stage. I watch as Allegra bows, placing her hand over her heart, first in thanks to the crowd, then to the conductor. She tilts her head in the direction of the box, blowing us a kiss, then kissing her engagement ring, a gesture to me, telling me how much she loves me.

"Now what happens?" I ask aloud.

"The judges go backstage to decide the winners," Signora Pavoni informs us. "It takes some time, so the guest artist sings one aria to keep the audience occupied."

"How many winners are chosen?" Mr. Orsini wants to know.

"Five or six out of the ten finalists. Allegra has some competition, but that one mezzo-soprano—"

"*Dio mio!* She was horrible!" La Diva declares.

Luciana, Tomas, and Signora Pavoni all nod their heads in agreement. We fall into a hush as the guest artist, a tenor, is introduced to sing an aria from *Tosca*.

While the others sit in their seats rapt in attention, I can't focus on anything. I pull out my phone to text Allegra. I know she won't be checking her phone. She's probably pacing the floor backstage with the other finalists. But I type out a text anyway:

You were amazing, baby! You fucking OWNED that stage! I am so proud of you! I love you so damn much!

Finally, the tenor finishes and bows to the crowd. He joins the host at the podium and starts a light banter with him to kill time while we await the judges' decision. What they're saying is all white noise to me. Allegra has to win. She just *has* to. The only time I wanted something to happen this badly was when I begged for Allegra to be rescued when that asshole Morandi kidnapped her.

A man suddenly steps out from the wings and hands a folded piece of paper to the host. The crowd falls silent. The winners, the host announces, will be read in no particular order.

A tenor and countertenor are declared winners, followed by a soprano, a bass-baritone, and another tenor.

One more name. My knees begin to jump nervously. Allegra's father grabs my arm, clamping onto it like a vise.

Please God, let it be Allegra. Please, please, please.

"Allegra Orsini!"

I scream, "YES!" as I shoot to my feet, joined by the rest of Allegra's loved ones. We hoot and holler for her and cry openly, probably violating every ounce of Metropolitan Opera House decorum, but none of us gives a shit. With La Diva in my box, we are bona fide and nobody would dare tell us to settle down.

Allegra steps forward to take a bow, blowing all of us a kiss. She joins the other winners for a mutual bow, then the other finalists come out together one last time as they all join hands and acknowledge the applause from the audience, walking off into the wings together.

I smile as all I hear around me is sniffling, watching as La Diva digs out tissues and hands them to everyone to wipe the happy tears from their faces. We start gathering our things to go to the private reception for the finalists one floor above on the Grand Tier level.

A guard checks our passes as we walk into the roped-off area.

Waiters walk by with trays stacked with flutes of champagne, but just as I'm about to grab one, a rousing round of applause goes up from the guests as the winners enter the party. Allegra spots us right away and runs over to us. Her father is closest to her and embraces her tightly, kissing her on both cheeks. They exchange animated words in Italian as La Diva and Signora Pavoni join in, hugging and kissing her.

I patiently wait my turn to be with her, but I don't have to for much longer, because I spot her scanning the room, and finally, she reaches my gaze, her face breaking into a huge smile, fresh tears appearing in her eyes when she sees me. We quickly make our way over to each other, reaching our arms out and immediately clamping our mouths on each other, kissing long and deep. I don't give a fuck if anyone is staring. This is my woman, who just won a major prize in the opera world, and I am so fucking proud of her.

When we pull back, she hugs me firmly, nestling her head in the crook of my neck.

"I saw your text, Harvard," she whispers into my ear.

"I didn't think you'd have time to read it."

"I was getting nervous waiting backstage after I finished, so I fixed my makeup and checked my phone. Sorry I didn't reply."

I rear back in astonishment. "Baby, you have nothing to apologize for. I just wanted you to know I was thinking of you, but I always am."

She smiles sweetly at me. "I know, Davison."

Our private moment is interrupted by Luciana, who slams into Allegra, practically tackling her. "Oh my God, Alli! You were amazeballs! I'm so proud of you!"

Allegra reaches for my hand once she unwraps herself from Luciana's embrace. "Thanks! I was so nervous singing the first aria, but then when I sang Mimi, I just knew I'd nailed it."

"You totally did! And that mezzo was hideous!"

Allegra looks around her. "Christ, Lucy!" she hisses. "She might be around here somewhere."

"Who gives a shit? She lost and you won," Luciana replies, blunt as ever.

Tomas comes over to join us. He gives Allegra a congratulatory hug, then Luciana instantly wraps her arm around him and gives him a quick kiss on the lips.

"We have the best news," she announces. "Can I tell them?"

"As if I could stop you," he answers her with a smile.

I can't help but smirk.

That boy is whipped. And I should know. Allegra's done the same to me.

"Tomas is going to debut in a featured role in *Don Giovanni* at the Prague State Opera, and I'm going with him!" she announces.

Our mouths drop at her news. I hold out my hand to Tomas. "Congratulations. Allegra and I will have to come to Prague to see you on opening night," I tell him.

He nods in appreciation. "I *vould* like that very much, Mr. Berkeley."

"And while we're in Europe, we're going to travel and I'm going to audition for lots of festivals and opera companies," Luciana adds to her big news. "Tomas and I are compiling an itinerary already, and I want your input too, Alli."

"That's great, Lucy! Of course I'll help." Allegra hugs her. "We need to get together before you leave anyway, for one last celebration."

"Definitely," she replies excitedly.

As much as I don't mind her friends' company, I need to be alone with Allegra because I have something I need to show her.

"Would you mind terribly if I drag Allegra away for a moment?" I interrupt.

"Of course we don't," Luciana replies, winking at me.

Oh, for fuck's sake.

I grab Allegra, pulling her behind me, avoiding every person who wants her attention. I refuse to stop for anyone.

I quickly make our way down the red carpeted stairs to the ground floor.

"Hey, Harvard, would you mind slowing down? These aren't exactly ballet flats I'm wearing," she remarks in reference to her black stiletto heels, of which I took great notice while she was onstage.

"Almost there," I reply over my shoulder.

I guide us around the throng of people in the lobby, exiting through the glass doors. I head straight for the black marble fountain in the center of the plaza.

"Okay, Davison." She huffs out of breath. "First of all, I'm wearing a gown and I'm freezing."

I remove my suit jacket and watch as she puts it on.

"That's a great look on you," I tell her admiringly.

She smiles as she crosses her arms and locks her eyes with mine. "Second, what's so important that you had to drag me out here to tell me when it's much warmer inside?"

I smirk as I step closer to her, brushing her right tit as I reach for the business card holder in the breast pocket of my jacket.

"Well, that was convenient," she remarks, watching my hand.

"Funny fiancée. I was getting this," I say as I hold up the metal object to her face.

"And what's inside there?" she asks curiously.

I pull a card out to show it to her. With a shit-eating grin, I watch as she reads the inscription—

THE DCB GROUP

DAVISON CABOT BERKELEY—CHAIRMAN AND CEO

Her eyes pop out as she takes it in. "Is this your new company?"

"Yup," I reply proudly.

"Oh my God, Davison, I'm so proud of you!" she screeches, jumping into my arms. "I knew you'd create one eventually, but I didn't want to be a nuisance and ask you when it would happen."

I rear back so I can look into her shining brown eyes. "Baby, you could never be a nuisance to me."

She pauses for a moment, as if she were heavy in thought. "What is it?" I ask worriedly.

"You know, this is where I ran to after I saw you with Ashton that night at the opera when I thought you had lied to me."

My heart drops at the mention of what happened after that night, the time when I thought I'd lost my chance with her. "Oh, Allegra, you don't have to think about that anymore," I tell her soothingly.

"No, Davison. I'm okay about it now, because this card," she says pointedly, waving it in the air to stress her point, "this card that represents a new chapter in your life, and it reminds me of the night we first met. The night you came to retrieve your lost driving glove from me, the one that has your initials stitched on it, just like this embossed card."

I stroke her cheeks tenderly with the pads of my thumbs. "We've really come full circle, haven't we, baby?"

She nods. "Yes, we have. And I'll always be grateful for taking the job over there at Le Bistro," she says, pointing at the legendary restaurant, across the street from Lincoln Center, "because otherwise we never would've met."

I smile. "Thank God for coat checks."

"Indeed." She steps forward and embraces me tightly. "I'm so proud of you, Davison."

"Just as I am of you, Venus."

I unwrap myself from her grasp, first reaching for her right hand to kiss the finger that's wearing the ruby ring I gave her in Venice, then her left one to run my lips over her ring finger, the one wearing my engagement ring.

"Like I said, my love…we're shatterproof."

Her eyes soften at my words. She leans in to kiss me fully and deeply as I quickly reciprocate. In the middle of the plaza, with the cacophony of the city that we love and that brought us together surrounding us, we kiss and kiss and kiss, oblivious to everything except each other.

Please turn the page for an excerpt of the first book in
Davison & Allegra's erotic romance

Breathless for Him

Available now!

Chapter One

T hank you. Enjoy the rest of your evening."

I watch as the last of the patrons don their camel-hair coats and calf-length sable furs. Before they leave, the owner makes sure to shake each of their hands. As they exit, the black velvet curtain that covers the front door swishes like a whisper against the marble floor, shielding the interior of the restaurant from the chilly November air. They shuffle their way out to begin the search for their town cars, a fleet of which stand outside on Broadway, engines idling, waiting to be claimed.

I'm standing inside my work space, which happens to be the coat-check room of Le Bistro, a restaurant that is an institution on the Upper West Side of Manhattan. Like Sardi's in the Theater District, Le Bistro is its equivalent, except it serves the opera buffs, cineastes, and ballet lovers of Lincoln Center. Its owner is Elias Crawford, one of New York City's most well-known restaurateurs, known for his charm, sophistication, and meticulous attention to detail.

Dressed in my standard uniform of a white long-sleeved blouse with French cuffs, black trousers, and black ballet flats, my dark brown hair done up in its usual chignon, I turn and take in my surroundings. Technically, my work space is a closet, lined with clothing rods for coats and jackets and shelves for handbags and briefcases. Since I began working there, I have checked an eclectic collection of items, from a famous rock star's red leather jacket pockmarked with cigarette burns to a vintage Louis Vuitton trunk that took up most of the traffic pattern.

Lola, the statuesque hostess, pokes her head in the door. "We're done, Allegra. You can start closing up."

I nod. I begin to wrap the plastic check numbers in an elastic band, stowing them into the shoe box that I use as a Lost and Found. I count my tips and tuck them into my purse.

As I take one last survey of the room, I spot two objects on the floor. One is a black-and-white silk scarf, the name "Hermès" imprinted in the lower right-hand corner.

The other is a man's driving glove, brown lambskin, cashmere-lined, with initials stitched on the inseam—DCB.

I stow both items in my Lost and Found shoe box. Perhaps the owners will collect them in the next few days.

* * *

"Did you hear about Davison's latest venture? He's flying to China to check out some new company that's doing amazing stuff with voice technology."

"Ha! 'Voice technology,' my ass! The only voice he's concerned about getting away from belongs to that shrew girlfriend of his, Ashton. She's got a hot body, but she's a total bitch—at least that's what I've heard."

That's what gossip is to me. Hearsay. It's common for someone to approach me while I'm working, offering me monetary compensation for any kernel of gossip that involves a celebrity. Because of its trendy status and location, Le Bistro attracts everyone from politicians to film stars to opera divas, basically anyone who's ever appeared in *Vanity Fair*. I knew since I began working here six months ago that if someone really wanted the truth about a scandal, the people to eavesdrop on were the doctors and lawyers who came into the restaurant. But I treat my place of work as a confessional; whatever I overhear will never be passed on to a third party.

The two men retrieving their coats are discussing the couple whose names and faces were featured almost every day on Page Six—Davison Cabot Berkeley, the Manhattan billionaire and heir to the Berkeley Holdings fortune, and Ashton Lane Canterbury, the heiress of the Canterbury family. Since they're the "it couple" of Manhattan, their histories are well known thanks to the tabloids and business pages. They're childhood friends. He has the proper pedigree: age thirty-one, prepped at Exeter, undergrad and MBA from Harvard, while she went to Miss Porter's and Wellesley.

A match made in WASP heaven.

It's funny, though, because every time I see their photo in the paper, she always looks much happier than he does, as if he would rather be anyplace else than with her. My life is far removed from the circles they travel in, but seeing such a handsome man so miserable with the woman he supposedly loves, I wonder if he is truly in love with her. I'm twenty-four, a butcher's daughter, but I don't envy their social or financial status in society.

I'm putting away the men's tips in my purse when a sharp knock on the flat ledge of the coat-check room's half door brings me back to the present moment.

"Excuse me? Are you working or not?"

At the door stands a tall woman with platinum-blonde hair that cascades down the back of her fur coat, a black crocodile Birkin hanging in the crook of her elbow.

"I said, did you happen to find a black-and-white Hermès scarf two nights ago?" her voice shrills above the cacophony of the restaurant. Her thin, oval-shaped face holds an exasperated look, while her blue eyes burn my face like a set of lasers.

"I did. Just a moment, I'll retrieve it for you."

As I pull out the Lost and Found box, I hear the woman speaking to her female entourage. "Oh my God, Davis is the biggest nerd. He never wants to go out. All he wants to do is stay home and read books or watch movies. He's *so* boring." She sighs. "But at least we're going away for the holidays to his family's chalet in Gstaad. I can't wait to see his new jet. We have invitations to *so* many parties when we're there."

Suddenly, I know whose scarf I'm holding. It belongs to the shrew herself, Ashton Canterbury.

Ashton's friends giggle in enchantment over the gilded life she is supposedly leading.

I walk back to Ashton with scarf in hand. I observe her, concluding that the tabloid photos actually make her look better than she does in person.

"Took you long enough," she huffs. "I hope nothing's happened to it."

"It's in pristine condition, madam. I kept it safe," I reassure her.

"Yes, well, it looks fine. Let's go, girls."

The lack of a gratuity from her does not come as a surprise to me.

* * *

"*O mio babbino caro?*"

Two days later during the lunch service, I'm bent over picking some dust off the floor humming the aria to myself when a deep male voice interrupts me.

I'm still distracted when I reply to the man. "Yes, how did you know?"

"My family has a private box at the Met."

When I stand up and turn to the door, I see in front of me what no photo could ever do any justice, now that Davison Cabot Berkeley is standing in front of me. He has to be over six feet tall, with dark brown wavy hair that borders on black. His eyes are deep green with flecks of amber in them. On any other man, his lips would look odd because of their lush shape, but on his chiseled face, they are perfectly suited.

He's dressed in a navy-blue wool coat, open to reveal underneath it a dark gray pin-striped suit and tie, accentuated by a button-down shirt in a lighter palette. A cashmere scarf the same shade as his coat is tied around his neck.

His eyes meet my dark brown ones, and in a flash, my throat goes dry. Shivers run up and down my arms. My pulse increases because of the way he stares at me. His head rears back slightly, and he takes in a deep breath through his aquiline nose. But it's the intensity of his eyes that paralyzes me. They sear me, as if they have the ability to read my inner thoughts without having to speak a word.

After a few seconds that seemed more like a full minute, I clear my throat. "You're very fortunate. May I be of service, sir?"

A small grin appears on his face. "Yes. I seem to have misplaced a glove. By any chance, would you happen to have found it?"

"I believe so. Could you describe it?"

"Brown driving glove, cashmere lined. My initials are on it. DCB. Davison Cabot Berkeley."

The sound of his voice warms my body, as if it were a cashmere blanket that tightly wraps around me. When he speaks, he speaks deeply, but it's more like a rumble, as if something is inside him on the verge of erupting. Even though he's only spoken a few words to me, I have a vision of him commanding others with that voice, and how intimidated I would feel, which is actually beginning to happen to me at that precise moment.

All I can do is nod my head. "Yes. I have it. I'll be right back."

As I turn to retrieve the Lost and Found shoe box, he says, "You have a lovely voice."

Thankfully, I'm looking away from him when he says that because as soon as he does, my face turns hot. "Thank you, but I was just humming, sir."

"I can still tell, though. Are you a singer?"

My face now cooling down, I finally turn around. "Yes, I am actually. I'm a graduate student of voice at the Gotham Conservatory."

"Opera?"

"Yes."

"So I suppose the fact that you work across from one of the most famous opera houses in the world is not a coincidence?" His lips lift in a sly grin.

I laugh slightly from my nerves. "No, it is not."

He smiles at me. "Umm, may I..." he asks, gesturing to the glove in my hand.

I shake my head in embarrassment. "Oh, I'm sorry. Of course."

He takes the glove from me, running his fingers over the stitched initials. "Hmm. I wonder..."

"About what, sir?"

"I wonder when my parents named me if their goal was to see how many surnames they could slap on their newborn child."

I smile, laughing slightly. "I can imagine."

His head tilts at me curiously as he leans in closer to me. "What's your name?"

I swallow in my throat as his warm breath caresses my face. "Allegra."

"Allegra what?"

"Allegra Orsini."

He pauses for a moment. "That's a lovely name. Italian?"

"Yes, sir."

I look into his eyes, which are still boring into mine. I can't move. Something is...there. Something...powerful. It takes my breath away. We both seem to be stunned into silence.

He pushes back the tail of his coat to retrieve something from his pocket. He pulls out his wallet and shuffles through the bills.

A fifty-dollar bill appears on the flat ledge of the door.

I push the money back to him. "No, that's not necessary."

"Please take it. It's not just for the glove. It's been a long time since…I just want you to have it."

"Truly, I can't accept it. For the same reason."

He nods in understanding. He puts his hand over mine, the hand that's trying to return the money to him. He doesn't move, and neither do I.

Without warning, he begins rubbing his thumb over my hand, slowly. So slowly. My breaths begin to increase. His emerald eyes turn darker, hooded with a look that both scares me and arouses me. The warmth from his touch permeates my skin, setting the rest of me aflame. I can feel myself turning wet at the apex of my thighs. I press my lips together, determined not to break this moment. He is powerful and commanding. I can't look away. And I don't want to.

Then he moves in closer to me. His lush mouth opens to say something, his thumb still moving again and again over my hand.

"Do you think I could make you come just by doing this?"

"What?" I manage barely above a whisper.

"Answer the question," he commands huskily.

Before I can answer him, a cell phone begins to ring inside his coat, which effectively breaks the moment. I step back as he shuts his eyes, emitting a low growl, then pulls out the phone, grimacing when he checks the caller ID. He lets it continue to ring as he shoves it back into his coat.

He pauses a moment, then takes the fifty and returns it to his wallet. Like a magician, he then reveals the glove's mate from his coat, and I watch him put on both of them.

His hands now fully gloved, he looks at me again, both of his green eyes fixed onto my own. They seem darker, ominous almost.

I swallow. "Have a good evening, sir."

He leans into my space, mere inches from me. His scent, something laundered with a hint of spice permeates my nose, his hot breath caressing my face once more. "Good night, Allegra."

Once Davison Cabot Berkeley leaves, shaking Mr. Crawford's hand on the way out, I step into a corner of the coat-check room, leaning against it in the darkness. I press my head against the wall as I try to catch my breath.

No man has ever affected me like that before, mostly because I would never allow it. I know it was just a moment. That's what I tell myself. We will never see each other again. And it's just as well, because I never let in a man far enough to know my deepest secrets.

About the Author

Sofia Tate grew up in Maplewood, New Jersey, the oldest of three children in a bilingual family. She was raised on '70s disaster films and '80s British New Wave music and classic TV miniseries. Her love for reading started when she received a set of Judy Blume books from her aunt when she was ten. She discovered erotic romance thanks to Charlotte Featherstone. She loves both writing and reading erotic romance. She graduated from Marymount College in Tarrytown, New York, with a degree in international studies and a minor in Italian. She also holds an MFA in Creative Writing from Adelphi University. She has lived in London and Prague. Sofia currently resides in New York City.

Learn more at:
 sofiatate.com
 Twitter: @sofiatateauthor
 Facebook: Sofia Tate
 Pinterest: Sofia Tate
 Goodreads: Sofia Tate